The Mentor

The Mentor
Shaping a New Generation

Robert Day Potter

Ephesus Press
Hillsboro WI

Ephesus Press
Hillsboro WI 54634
www.nurembergreflections.com

Ephesus Press is a trademark of Robert Day Potter.

The text of this book is set in 12pt Minion Pro.

ISBN-13: 978-0-615-67718-7
ISBN-10: 0-615-67718-5

Printed in the United States of America

First Edition
August 2012
18 17 16 15 14 13 12   1 2 3 4 5

Contents

Preface 1

Chapter One: "Nein" 3

Chapter Two: The Long, Dark Journey Inward 9

Chapter Three: Monk, My Mentor................................ 23

Chapter Four: The Hangman 37

Chapter Five: The Warrior Within 51

Chapter Six: The Werkmeister.................................... 56

Chapter Seven: The Magician Within............................ 72

Chapter Eight: How I Met My King................................ 77

Chapter Nine: Pursuit of a Tyrant 92

Chapter Ten: Triumph of the King 97

Chapter Eleven: The King Within.................................. 101

Chapter Twelve: The Lover 105

Chapter Thirteen: The Dark Side 114

Chapter Fourteen: Finding My Father 122

Chapter Fifteen: A Vision of Heaven 128

Chapter Sixteen: Final Exams 135

Chapter Seventeen: The Light 138

Chapter Eighteen: A Second Chance 141

Chapter Nineteen: The Final Word 148

Afterword 153

Ode to a Cottonwood Tree 155

Acknowledgements 157

For Further Reading 159

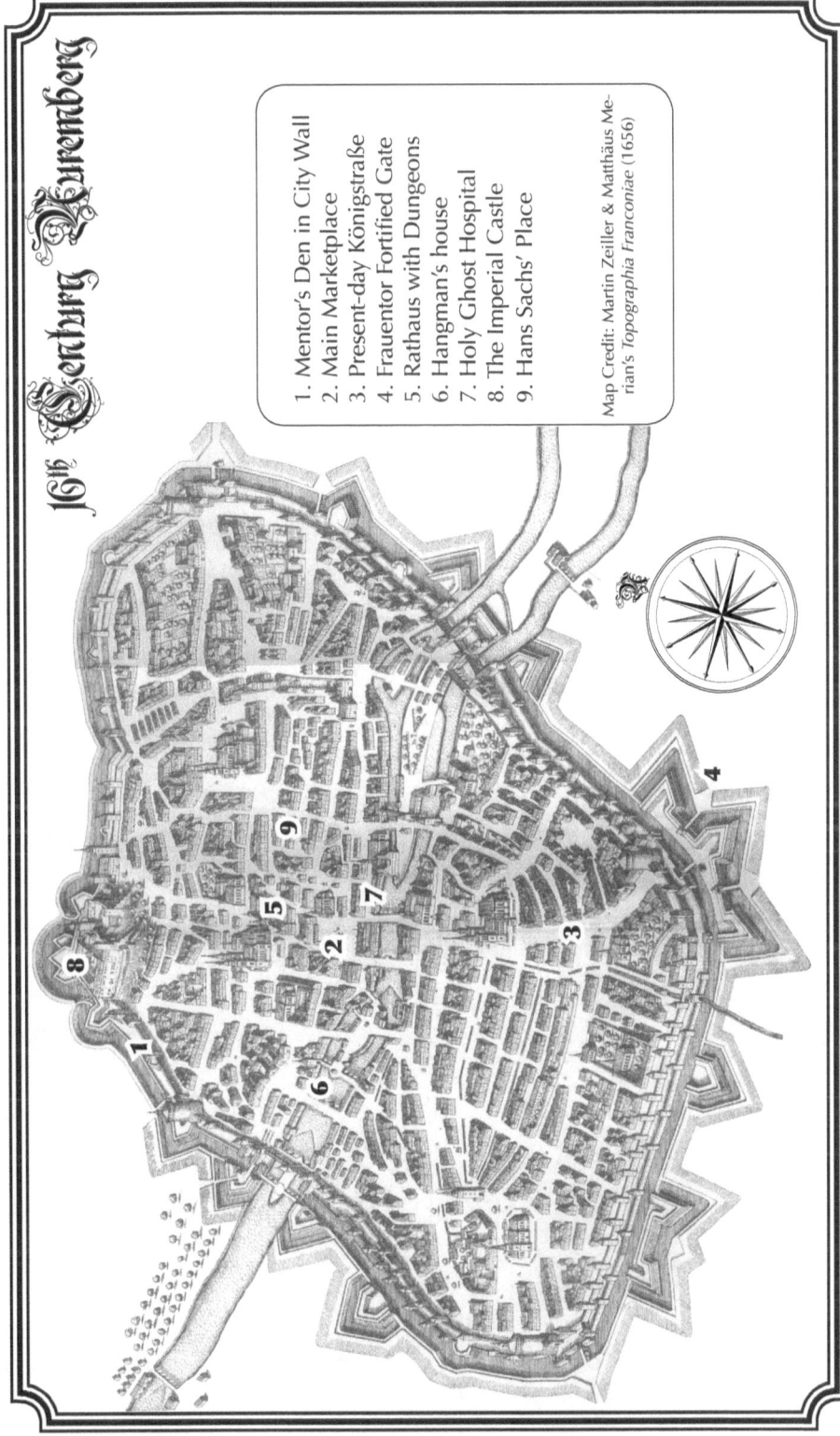

16th Century Nuremberg

1. Mentor's Den in City Wall
2. Main Marketplace
3. Present-day Königstraße
4. Frauentor Fortified Gate
5. Rathaus with Dungeons
6. Hangman's house
7. Holy Ghost Hospital
8. The Imperial Castle
9. Hans Sachs' Place

Map Credit: Martin Zeiller & Matthäus Merian's *Topographia Franconiae* (1656)

Preface

A pair of hikers climbed the Hemlock Trail in Wildcat Mountain State Park. The young man heard his grandfather panting as they neared the summit of Mount Pisgah and spotting a bench said, "Whew, I need a break. Mind if we sit?"

The old man lowered himself onto the varnished oaken slab with the aid of his hiking stick. "No problem, Alex. You're probably not used to this. Too many hours playing computer games."

"Yeah Grandpa," Alex smiled. They gazed at the valley below, a great expanse of various shades of green, tinged with gold, crimson, and umber—the colors of early autumn in Wisconsin. A large, dark bird soared one hundred yards in the distance. "Eagle?" Alex asked.

"Turkey vulture," said the old man, "about six foot wingspan."

"Wow!" said Alex. He plucked a sprig of goldenrod, just to have something to fiddle with.

"Crush the leaves and smell them, Alex," said the old man.

"Hmm…smells something like that black hard candy…"

"Anise."

"Yeah."

"It's sweet goldenrod, Alex. You can make a tea out of the leaves and flowers."

"Really? Is it any good?"

"It's okay I guess."

"Grandpa, you've turned into a wild man of the woods since you retired to Wisconsin. How did you get so smart?"

"Oh, I hang around with smart people. You know, the people in Hillsboro are a lot smarter than the people in Chicago."

"Oh yeah? How so?" He and his grandpa were like buddies; they liked to kid each other.

"Well, for one thing, everyone in Hillsboro knows where Chicago is, but no one in Chicago knows where Hillsboro is."

Alex laughed. He stood and leaned on the rail fence guarding the edge of the overlook. When he turned to face his grandfather, his eyes were shining. He spoke softly and earnestly, as if in prayer on a hilltop chapel: "Grandpa, we're in love." Then his voice quavered with excitement: "I'm going to ask her to marry me."

The old man felt a tightness around his eyes, his throat, and his chest. He raised his arms to embrace his grandson. There they remained, united by the long trail they had climbed together, by twenty-one years of love, and by the boundless horizon ahead.

The young man held his grandfather at arm's length and looked deeply into his eyes. "I just want to make her happy, Grandpa."

The old man returned his grandson's expectant gaze. "I know you do, Alex, and I believe you will. If I were a wise old wizard, and I could simply hand you a book of magic spells—sort of a cookbook for life, I would certainly do that. As it happens, however, each of us has to try a little of this, a little of that, taste it, and hope we don't poison our loved ones."

"I'm scared, Grandpa; I don't want to hurt her. How can I know if I'm ready for this?"

"You must know this, Alex; you have all the ingredients, all the magic you need. They are inside you: a Warrior, to protect your loved ones; a Magician, to guide you to the secret knowledge you must master to provide for your family; a King, to lead others in worthy quests; and a Lover, to animate and fulfill your relationships. You must meet these inner teachers and learn your lessons well before you step off this mountain."

"But Grandpa, how do I meet them?"

"I will make the introductions, Alex, by telling you how I met my own four teachers when I was about your age. I have never told this story to anyone before, but I love you and I trust you. I have known you for twenty-one years, and I believe you are ready to hear this amazing story."

"I would like that, Grandpa."

CHAPTER ONE

"Nein"

"Nein."

That word broke my heart, Alex. It means "no" in German, and it came from the lips of the person who mattered most to me—the woman who had given happiness, hope, and love to a homesick, clueless G.I.

I was really sick of the Army by the second year of my hitch. "Mickey Mouse" inspections, K.P. duty, and spot painting my deuce-and-a-half in the motor pool every day made me feel like a moron. Living with a few thousand other morons who amused themselves after hours by getting drunk and fighting was wearing me down. I had lost all self-confidence, avoiding contact with other G.I.s as much as possible. I simply counted down the days until my hitch was up with no real plan for the future. I was a mess.

Then I met her—Gerdi.

It was a Sunday, the fourth of July, 1965. The Army magnanimously issued passes that day in honor of Independence Day, so Johnson, Boone, and I took a walk. "Let's check out the rally grounds," someone said.

We were stationed in the *SS Kaserne* in Nürnberg, Germany. It was an impressive bit of architecture. Rumor had it that there were tunnels leading from the lowest level of the *SS Kaserne* to other parts of the city, including the Nazi party rally grounds a few blocks away. That's where hoards of Hitler lovers from all over Germany came to hear their *Führer* in the 1930s.

When we passed the *Kongreßhalle* (Congress Hall), another Nazi pipedream, and drew closer to the rally grounds, we could hear crowds of cheering Germans. We exchanged glances; what was going on over there? Was it a neo-Nazi thing, a reenactment of the political rallies three decades earlier? "Them Germans sound pretty excited," said Boone, "I reckon we should hang back and scope things out before we get too close."

As we drew nearer, however, we saw that this was a rally of a different sort—a road rally. The wide street where Hitler's fanatical supporters had once marched past his reviewing stand was blocked off with high chain-link fences, and the concrete stands were packed with Germans indulging one of their modern national passions—fast cars.

The three of us watched racecars roar around the grandstand for a few minutes, but then we wandered off to the park-like *Dutzendteitch* to escape the noise and crowds. We came to a part of the *Große Straße* ("Great Street" intersecting the rally grounds) fenced off by the U.S. Army for use as a military airstrip. Even here, the former parade route was lined with concrete benches, apparently placed there in the 1930s for spectators to view formations of soldiers, work corps, and youth groups as they marched by. We spotted a young German lady seated on one of these benches, her bicycle parked before her. She was reading a book.

"A *hammer!*" remarked Johnson. ("Hammer" was a term used by "colored"—later referred to as "Black," then "Afro," and still later, "African-American" G.I.s. to designate potentially available German girls.)

Concerned that these horny G.I.s would besmirch the already-tarnished reputation of my countrymen, I ordered them to stand down. (As a Specialist Four, I was, after all, the ranking member of our trio.) Johnson and Boone walked on, and I sat on the concrete slab a few yards from the *Fräulein*—her protector.

I listened to my transistor radio and puzzled about how I might strike up a conversation with the pretty young lady. Having had no experience with this sort of thing, it required a few minutes of consideration. We had something in common, I noted, for I had recently purchased a bicycle myself, at the *Fahrrad Fuchs* bike shop in Nürnberg. I also enjoyed reading. Wouldn't it be nice to meet a Fräulein while I was in Germany, to gain a first-hand perspective on the culture and perhaps advance my facility in the German language beyond G.I. slang? Surely no harm could come from a casual German-American acquaintance. "I'll ask her the time," I thought, spotting her wristwatch. "That is innocent enough, and perhaps she doesn't know enough English to realize that the Armed Forces Network playing on my transistor radio announces the time every few minutes." Searching my memory for the correct phrase, I said, *"Entschuldigen sie bitte, Fräulein, wieviel Uhr ist es?"* (Excuse me, miss, what time is it, please?). Without looking up from her book, she thrust out her arm in my direction so that I could read her watch. It was not exactly a receptive response to my advance, but at least she did not hop on her bike and speed off—or scream, "Get lost!"

"Danke schön," I said. Following a few more minutes of pretending to listen to my radio (and her pretending to read), I gestured to her bicycle and informed her that I, too, enjoy bike riding. That must have made me seem fairly harmless, for we then attempted a hybrid conversation of German and English. Before long, she announced that she had to be going, but she walked her bike, allowing me to accompany her. It was unseasonably cool, so I attempted to place my jacket over her. In retrospect, that was a rather bold thing to do. She must have thought so as well, for she refused the gesture with a slightly annoyed twist of her shoulders. "This is a girl with spunk," I thought.

As we neared the SS Kaserne and the parting of our ways, my desperation to see her again impelled me to make another bold move. "Will you have dinner with me this evening?" I asked.

She agreed to meet me at the hotel formerly known as the *Deutscher Hof,* near the *Bahnhof* (train station). This grand edifice had been Hitler's quarters when he visited Nürnberg. Following the war, it was taken over by the U.S. military and was known to G.I.s as "The Army Hotel." It offered the best American-style restaurant in town, which is why I suggested it. Now that we had agreed to have a date (my first ever!), she told me her name—Gerdi.

I recall two things about that dinner date: one was romantic, and the other was funny.

First, from a grand piano in the elegant dining room came notes of a familiar tune—"I left my heart/In San Francisco..." I looked across the table at Gerdi; she recognized the song as well. I asked myself, "Will we ever ride the cable cars together?"

Second, as an American-run facility, the Army Hotel instructed its waiters to automatically place glasses of water before diners. This custom is unknown in European restaurants. When our water arrived, Gerdi asked what it was.

"American beer," I replied. She looked askance at the pale liquid.

When I raised my glass and said, *"Prost!"* Gerdi took a sip. *"Das is Wasser!"* she laughed, "This is water!"

When, not long after that fateful day, Gerdi and I walked in the city park, sat on a bench, and kissed—really kissed—I fell in love. Gerdi had kissed me, despite my harelip! Could this be my chance for happiness? I was delirious, ecstatic, head over heels in love. My life, my future was with Gerdi. I was sure of it. But was she?

With just over six months remaining on my enlistment, I had to act fast. We went for bike rides in the country, for long walks in the city, holding hands and using a strange system to communicate. With my free hand, I thumbed a tiny *Langerscheidt* German-English dictionary to understand her as she spoke German to me, and I answered in English. We sometimes drew the stares of people in restaurants or streetcars, but like young lovers the world over, we were oblivious to others.

We got together whenever I could score a pass, and sometimes when I couldn't. The view of my room at the SS Kaserne was obscured from the front gate because the building jutted in from the street at that point. The unit police there couldn't see anyone scaling the barbed wire fence and traversing the ledge from it to my window. That fact had been a source of great consternation to me for the past two years, for drunken G.I.s regularly used my room to sneak in after bed check, disturbing my sleep. Now, however, when I could not get a pass, my strategic location proved a blessing.

I even found a way to communicate with Gerdi during field maneuvers. I recall stuffing my sleeping bag after an all-night shift in the radio rig, creeping out of my pup tent, and making my way through the woods in full combat regalia to a nearby village. The *Frau* who owned the village *Gasthaus* was startled when I entered, but she helped me make the telephone call to Gerdi's office at *Kabel- und Metallwerke Neumeyer AG*. Like the other female operators who patched me through to Gerdi's office, she seemed excited to facilitate such a romantic connection. Even Frau Schmidt, Gerdi's dour coworker, giggled when she handed the receiver to Gerdi. If this episode had been part of a Hallmark movie, the urgent message would have been a proposal of marriage. Alas, the "secret mission" was motivated only by a lovesick G.I.'s need to hear his *Schatzie's* voice.

My twenty-first birthday in August and Gerdi's twenty-fifth birthday in November were reminders that our carefree state of bliss was not sustainable. Gerdi knew that I was smitten, and she enjoyed my adoration, but it troubled her.

Her *"Tweety"* was a nice boy, but he was a *boy*. She needed a *man*—a man who had a clear vision of his future, a man whom she could follow on his quest for that future. She needed a strong man, a man who would fight for himself—and for her. She needed a man who would fight *with* her, when necessary, and not always agree with her as this nice boy did. She needed a man who would conquer his world by seeking to understand it—a man for whom knowledge is power. Most of all, she needed a man who would love her—really love her—not just in a sappy, romantic movie way, but the way her grandfather had loved her. This American boy—Bob—was infatuated with her, but would he be as devoted to her when the good times turned to real life? Would he hold her when she cried? Would he listen to her? Would he love her when she was bitchy? Would he sacrifice to make a good home for their family? Would he want her—and only her—when she gained weight, when she got wrinkles, when her hair turned gray? Would he love her enough to fight with her? Would he lie with her at the end? Would this boy—this adoring boy who was so much fun when they went out for chicken dinner at the *Wienerwald* restaurant, when they named the giraffe at the *Tiergarten* "Tweety," when they rode their bikes to a secret picnic spot in the woods—be man enough for her?

"Nein." That is what Gerdi told me when I proposed to her in November. I was not ready, she told me; I had a life back home, she told me. I had to find myself first, and then find a mate for life, she told me. Yes, she loved me, she said, but there is so much more to marriage than the kind of carefree infatuation that I was feeling. Yes, we had much in common, she said, but we were from different worlds. She had grown up in the ashes of bombed-out Nürnberg, she said; she had to pick among the rubble for scraps of food. She had to listen to her teachers, despite the gnawing hunger in her belly, to learn the lessons of survival in a tough world. She had to study the basics: math, science, grammar, history, and the skills needed to help rebuild her country: English, shorthand, typing, and office administration. Every person in Germany had to pick a trade or profession early and stick with it; it was the only way.

"You," she told me, "grew up in a land of plenty: cars, television, too much food, too much fun—you don't know hardship, so you think everything is possible. I love you, *Tweety*, but marriage...*nein*."

A nice boy, but not quite a man

CHAPTER TWO

The Long, Dark Journey Inward

The weird part of this story starts on December 24, 1965. I'm sure of that, Alex, because I remember thinking how unfair it was that I had to pull K.P. duty on Christmas Eve. It was my last year in the Army, maybe my last chance to celebrate Christmas with Gerdi.

I had joined the Army after graduating from high school. Not that I was "gung-ho" about being a soldier; it was simply the best option at the time. The economy had been slow in 1962, and jobs were scarce in my steel mill neighborhood on the South Side, especially for men of draft age. Sending me to college was not an option for my widowed mother. She didn't earn much as a waitress. When she was off work due to illness, which was often, our only income was the proceeds from my door-to-door sales and a small widow's pension. The recruiting sergeant said that the Army would take care of my room and board, send an additional allotment to my mother, along with my what they took from my pay, and let me choose the theater of operations in which to serve: Stateside, Asia, or Europe.

So that's how I came to be scrubbing floors in the mess hall of Merrill Barracks in Nürnberg, Germany. The Germans called it the "SS *Kaserne.*" Built for Hitler's elite *Schutzstaffel,* it was adjacent to the parade grounds where thousands of people from all over Germany gathered in the 1930s to hear and see their *Führer.* Soldiers, youth organizations, unemployed workers, and other groups of Hitler supporters paraded past the man they believed would lead them to a brighter future. They marched on the *"Große Straße,"* the "Great Street," that Nazi architects deliberately aligned with the venerable Nürnberg castle, hoping that the city's historic prestige would rub off on their regime. As you know, Alex, Germany did not have a bright future under Hitler. The "Große Straße" became a landing strip for the U.S. Army after the war. I sometimes pulled guard duty there.

On one such occasion, startled by the sound of an approaching aircraft, I scrambled from the cab of a deuce-and-a-half truck where I had been dozing and raced across the concrete in my "Mickey Mouse boots." I wanted to appear vigilant when the pilot, undoubtedly an officer from my armored cavalry unit, landed. "Should I challenge this incoming plane?" I wondered. The general orders for a sentry stipulated that I should "…*challenge all persons on or near my post, and to allow no one to pass without proper authority.*" I took up a position in the center of the landing strip and yelled at the top of my lungs: "Halt!" The pilot continued his course; I chickened out. In my haste to get out of the plane's path, I slipped on an icy patch, landing on the butt of my unloaded M-16 rifle, which promptly disassembled itself into three parts. The plane, a Mohawk used by the Second Armored Cavalry to monitor the Iron Curtain border area, taxied to a halt, and a young lieutenant sauntered past me, sniggering at my attempt to salute him while holding the pieces of my weapon in my left hand. I was some soldier!

It was, however, interesting to be stationed in Nürnberg. Hitler was a master of propaganda. His architecture was built oversized and grandiose to make his followers feel part of something important. The SS Kaserne, my home for almost three years, guarded the south end of *Allesbergerstrasse* like a football lineman, its two massive shoulders hunched over an arched entryway. Each wing of the main building was five floors above ground and five floors below. At least, that's what G.I.s were told by other G.I.s. We used only the first basement and sub-basement; any levels below that were off-limits. The walls were so thick that I could stretch out on the windowsill, spit-shining my boots and listening to the Armed Forces Network on my portable radio.

After fourteen hours of K.P. on that Christmas Eve in 1965, it was all I could do to drag myself back to my room. It was empty, as I expected. Garcia had gone home for Christmas. Johnson would be at the Enlisted Men's Club, drinking Heinikens with the other colored guys in the communications platoon. My third roommate, Porter, a fundamentalist Christian from the Bible Belt, would be at the base chapel for

Christmas Eve services. I was happy to be alone. Too exhausted to take off my greasy fatigue uniform, I removed my combat boots and lay on my bunk. My plan was to sleep through the next day.

I had just dozed off when a disturbance in the corridor roused me, ready for fight or flight. It was a gang of thugs from the infantry platoon attached to Headquarters Troop on their way to a night of drinking, fighting, and making life miserable for anyone they encountered. This time, they had apparently encountered a clerk, or other civilized member of our troop, whose plans for Christmas Eve did not include a rumble with drunken Army misfits. "I don't want to fight," he pleaded, in a frightened voice.

I opened my door. A dozen or more guys had the kid surrounded. He was on the floor. They were stomping him, kicking him in the stomach, in the head, as if to kill him. I didn't recognize the victim or any of the assailants. I closed my door, shaking with fear, rage, and self-disgust. Why didn't I jump in and help the guy? Growing up on the South Side, I had never backed down from a fight. But this was not a fight; this was not a couple of boys facing off to establish the pecking order in their gang. These were the Army's dregs, recruited from inner city ghettos, unqualified for any military schools. Of course they ended up in the infantry, where they could hone their fighting skills. There was a bunch of them, and they were drunk. What could I do? I grabbed my military "entrenchment tool," a shovel with a short folding handle. It was part of the gear issued to each G.I. and displayed on top of his wall locker when he was not in the field. It was also a lethal weapon if swung like a baseball bat. In frustration, I beat my wall locker with the entrenchment tool.

My door opened. One of the hoodlums appeared, his face contorted with aggression. "Who makin' all that mother fucking noise?" he demanded. I turned toward him, holding the entrenchment tool like a baseball bat, as if I would slice off his head. He backed up and closed the door.

I did not have time to consider my options. In seconds, my room would be filled with the bloodthirsty mob, and I would have to kill or be killed, probably both. I preferred neither. My room was on what the Germans call "the first floor," which is really eight or ten feet above the quadrangle where we stood in formation for reveille. I did not hesitate. I swung the windows open, left and right, scrambled over the wide sill, and dropped to the quadrangle in my stocking feet. The frozen concrete stung my feet, but I could think of only one thing—escape! Hearing the voices of my pursuers behind me, I took refuge in the sub-basement. A boarded-up stairwell marked "OFF LIMITS" caught my eye. In my desperation, I pried a 2x4 loose with my bare hands. I squeezed through the opening and crouched in the black stairwell.

"That motherfucker done hatted up!"

"Shit, he gone cryin' to mama."

"Ain't no Commo mofo gonna mess with the L.R.R.P.!"

"L.R.R.P." was the Long-Range Reconnaissance Patrol, Alex.

"He gone; fuck the motherfucker!"

"Let's hit the strasse, man; I'm gonna get me a hammer."

"Shit, splib, you want some pussy, you gonna have to go to the wall!"

"Well then, I'll just take it!"

"You gonna have to kick some Komrade ass."

"Ain't no mofo Rad gonna mess with this splib!"

And then there was silence. I cowered in the dark stairwell long after my tormentors left. At first, all thought was displaced by numbing fear. Then, after what seemed an hour—in that darkness, a watch was useless—a quiet came over me. I felt strangely calm, isolated, as if my mother and my home in Chicago, my childhood, my stateside military training, even the world twenty feet above were scenes from an old movie, not my personal reality. Then I groped my way down the stairway and through the black corridor below as if I were seeking the solace of my mother's womb. Deprived of the ability to see, my consciousness became focused on my other senses. The fingertips of my right hand felt the wall, velvety with a thick layer of stale dust and cobwebs. I resisted the impulse to withdraw my hand, fearing that I would become disoriented. I was able to smell and taste the fine dust stirred up by my hand and my steps. I was able to hear my own breathing, the muffled scraping of bits of debris my bare feet contacted now and again as I shuffled through years of accumulated grit on the concrete floor. I heard what must have been the scurrying of a mouse. There, in that silent, subterranean darkness, on a Christmas Eve, I felt more alone, more vulnerable, and closer to God than ever before.

I hummed at first, then softly sang the words of an old hymn from my little Baptist church back home: *Have Thine own way, Lord, have Thine own way; I am the potter, Thou art the clay.*

Jesus, my closest childhood friend, spoke to me: "Lo, I am with you always, even unto the ends of the earth." Comforted by His words, and no longer afraid, I sat in the unseen layer of dust, my back supported by the wall, and contemplated the circumstances that had delivered me here—the end of the earth.

I hadn't known what to do with myself after graduation. College was for the other kids in my high school, the Jewish kids whose fathers were doctors, or lawyers, or who owned stores on 71st Street. Some of the token gentiles, members of the Chess Club, or Thespian Society, went away to the University of Illinois or Northwestern on the hard-earned savings of their dads. But those kids, Jews and gentiles, were different; their parents *expected* them to succeed. Their parents encouraged them to take physics, Latin, and calculus, not loser courses like salesmanship and business math. Even some of the other blue-collar kids, from south of 79th Street, with no extra-curricular activities listed after their photo in the yearbook, could take classes at the Pier or junior college. Their parents didn't understand, but they put up with it, as long as their son or daughter paid a little room and board out of earnings from a part-time job.

For me, it was different; the income from my door-to-door peddling had been the main source of support for my mother and me since my dad died when I was fifteen. Even though the income from that job sounded like a lot to Mr. Conrad, my salesmanship teacher, it did not compensate for the loss of Social Security survivor's benefits when I turned eighteen. I had to work full-time; college was not an option.

I told myself it didn't matter: "College is for rich snobs who just want to make a lot of money. Those kids don't care about knowledge for its own sake; they weren't sensitive, deep thinkers, who read the Bible every day and walked the length of South Park Avenue, just to prove that the colored wouldn't jump him."

But where could I get a job? The guard at the front gate of South Works steel mill, where my dad had worked, just laughed, "We got three thousand men on layoff now." The other factories on the Southeast Side were slow too. Besides, it was the depth of the Cold War, and I could be drafted any time.

So I kept going door-to-door with my cardboard box of merchandise: dish cloths, oven mitts, ironing board covers, dampening bags, all "processed-in-part or completely manufactured by blind or handicapped people." That's why people bought it—to help the handicapped, and sometimes, to help the pathetic kid standing on their doorstep in the rain or snow. Bob Kash worked one side of the street, and I worked the other. We stayed together, in case of trouble. You never could tell; we worked all over the South Side: Back-of-the-Yards, South Shore, Bridgeport, where the mayor lived. (But the cops who always parked in front of his house wouldn't let us go to his door.) We did get to "da mayor's" brother's house in Beverly, a ritzy neighborhood, however. The lady of the house was real pretty and nice, and she bought a package of four dishcloths for one dollar.

That same night, just a few blocks away, a kind lady invited me in out of the rain so she could take a look at my merchandise. There were several girls my age in the living room, dressed for a pajama party. Their giggling made my face red, so I kept looking down at the cardboard box in my arms as the mom decided what to buy. Then another girl, dressed in a feathered robe, descended a wide staircase to the living room, with the posture of a fashion model. One arm outstretched and nose pointed to the ceiling, she was blithely unaware of my presence. With a dramatic, "ta-dah!" she flung off her robe and posed, completely nude. The other girls, and even the mom, burst into hysteric laughter. Then the girl saw me, and ran, shrieking, upstairs again. The pajama party girls and their chaperone enjoyed the incident (and my discomfort) immensely. Did they know, I wondered, that this had been the first time I had ever seen a naked girl? Rich people were sure different from my blue-collar family.

Bob and I even tried selling in colored neighborhoods. We had no luck, even in upper-middle class areas of the South Side, where the famous musicians and ball players lived. I guess they didn't feel sorry for us.

The best territory was Pullman. The townhouses were really close together—no time wasted running between houses, and no talking through an intercom to get through the lobby door. Pullman has an interesting history, built as one of the first planned communities, by George M. Pullman, for his workers. The lavish Hotel Florence hosted executives and visiting dignitaries, and company stores served the needs of all employees, from supervisors, living in detached duplex units, to common laborers, housed in walk-up tenements. An elderly resident of one of these tenements told me about the strike of 1894, when the Army was called in to quell rioting by the workers. It had been one of his earliest memories. When Bob Kash and I met on the corner, we sat on a door stoop while I related the old man's tales of the "model town."

Selling door-to-door is mostly about walking up and down stairs ten hours a day, hearing "no," and having doors slammed in your face, like in the movies. Bob and I looked for any excuse to avoid work. We stopped in the middle of the day and drove to a new territory, the way fishermen move to a "better spot." We lingered over hamburgers and Cokes. Mostly, we sat in his Rambler and talked.

Religion was always good for an hour or two. We debated the fine points of his Catholicism versus my Baptist upbringing. Bob didn't know much about the Bible, but he had been an alter boy. The saints, the vestments of priests and nuns, and the rituals were pretty exotic stuff to me. Bob took me along when he attended St. Basil's and kidded me about my attempts to kneel, cross myself, and respond appropriately to the mass. The Latin mass had given way to Polish in his parish, but still, it was rich European rye, compared to the Wonder Bread of my pastor, with his blue suit and tie, and his plain English.

In October of that terrible year, Bob and I prayed together. The Russians were steaming toward our blockade of Cuba. Would the Titans clash, the Bomb fall, and our future be destroyed in a game of nuclear "chicken"? Why bother getting out of the Rambler and knocking on doors? The Russians turned around. Our prayers were answered.

One day, I was at a door with my box of merchandise, and a kind lady said, "I'll take a package of dish cloths. Wait here, and I'll be right back with the money." I could hear, through the open door, her asking her husband for a dollar, explaining that it was "for the handicapped." He asked if I was handicapped, and she replied, "Yeah, he has some kind of a speech thing."

"Handicapped?" Is that what I am? A speech defect is just a mechanical thing—an airflow problem, like a faulty damper in a heating duct. When you don't have a fully formed palate, air wants to escape through your nose. When your front teeth are missing, you do your best to form certain

sounds, but they don't come out right. It's a defective air duct, not a defective brain!

Yet, people judge what they hear. There is every reason, in a world where, "if you're not one up, you're one down," to look for weaknesses in others. Few kids wanted to play with me—none, when forced to choose between the dominant boys and me. One method employed to "ditch Bobby," when adventure beaconed, was to require each boy to utter a cuss word as initiation. Standing in a circle, each boy would, in turn, mouth the foulest word he could imagine. When it was my turn, they would all laugh, knowing that my Baptist restrictions (and Mom's tape playing in my brain) would leave me speechless.

Teachers, too, did their best to isolate me. It was uncomfortable to hear my malformed words, so they seldom asked me to recite. The music teacher frowned when her students were singing and walked to my desk. "Bobby, just move your mouth when we sing, but don't let any sound come out." I never sang in public again.

Introverted behavior, when forced upon a child, is unnatural, uncomfortable, but not without advantages. A boy without allies gets tough. Eventually, the other boys stopped trying to beat me up, a fact for which I was grateful, because I hated conflict. A boy without playmates learns to read, and to think.

The worst part about my birth defect was the harelip. It was called that because my upper lip, incompletely formed at birth, had to be sewn together, leaving it crooked, like a rabbit's. No girl would ever kiss those lips. No girl could ever stand to look at them. I didn't blame them; in fact, I helped them by averting my gaze. Still, I thought wistfully about how it must feel to kiss a girl, especially so pretty a girl as Marcia McGuire.

So I grew up alone, without parties or dates, without encouragement from teachers or parents. I was not smart, the way the Jewish kids in high school were smart, and I was not aggressive, but I could take care of myself.

Now, I heard, through the cracked door, that I was handicapped! Was being "handicapped" the real reason that no one would give me a job, and I had to peddle household items, processed in part, or completely manufactured by blind or handicapped people, door-to-door, and to hear a nice lady call me "handicapped"?

I looked in the telephone book, under "cleft palate." The Cleft Palate Institute of Northwestern University agreed to look at me, free of charge.

At the Institute, specialists in maxillofacial surgery, dentistry, speech therapy, and interns crowded around my open mouth as if it were an unearthed treasure. A few of the interns were pretty young ladies, not much older than I was. Someone noted that the repair had been good, and others murmured in agreement. An intern's long red hair brushed my face as she peered in. (It was, I am sorry to say, the most intimate moment I had shared with a young woman in my eighteen years.) Afterward, the head physician advised me that I would need surgery to extend my palate, a bridge to close the gap in my teeth, and an extended period of speech therapy. What kind of insurance did I have? No insurance? How would I pay the estimated $3,000? (That was 1962, when $3,000 would easily buy a new car.)

Mulling over that question, I took the elevator downstairs. From behind the front desk in the lobby, a voice startled me. I looked up, gesturing to myself, as if to ask, "Are you talking to me?"

"Yes, you," said a tall, wiry old gentleman, sporting a white beard and wearing the candy-striped shirt of a volunteer, "let me validate your parking pass." He looked like Uncle Sam saying, "I want you!"

"Of course!" I said aloud. It was the candy striper's turn to be startled. (I'm sure he thought that I had come from the psychiatric ward.) Uncle Sam wants me! And I need him—his three square meals and a place to sleep, a paycheck for Mom, and free dental care!

I tried the Marine Corps first. The few! The proud! The Marine Corps recruiter in South Chicago was doubtful. "You talk funny, kid." He made an appointment for me to be evaluated by a medical officer downtown.

The old Federal Building was a beautiful architectural landmark that would be razed in the 1960s to make room for a more efficient, ugly box. Parking downtown was a luxury I could ill afford on the slender proceeds of my door-to-door peddling, so I drove a couple miles west of the Loop until I found street parking on Taylor Street, an Italian neighborhood that was being torn down to make room for the University of Illinois campus. It was one of those minus twenty degree January days in Chicago.

When I finally stumbled, half frozen, into the Federal Building, it was time for my appointment. A major, who seemed to be expecting me, immediately handed me a newspaper and commanded me to read. My mouth, numb from the cold, would not respond. "Sorry son," the officer explained, "in the Marine Corps, everyone is potentially infantry. Your whole squad might be killed off, and you would have to pick up the radio and call for help. You couldn't do it."

The news was devastating to a boy who had grown up playing Marine. What now? I decided to try the Army. If they didn't take me, I reasoned, no one would. Classified 4-F, physically unfit for military service, I could go on with my life without the draft hanging over my head. Maybe the manager at the Jewel would let me stock groceries. I could take care of Mom, save to get my teeth fixed, maybe even take night classes at junior college. It wasn't much of a future, but it would have to be good enough for a kid who couldn't talk on the radio to save his life.

To make a long story short, I did try the Army. This time, I brought along my business partner, Bob, and our one remaining sales associate, Loren. The recruiting sergeant seemed pleased to see us. Signing up three recruits on the "buddy plan" would make his monthly quota easier to attain. He told us when and where to report for our physicals and told me to keep my mouth shut—just like my third grade singing teacher.

The "buddy plan" was to last only through basic training at Ft. Leonard Wood. One of the first rituals is the haircut. Bob and I laughed when Loren pretended to cry as the civilian barber shaved his head. He was a bit of a clown. Later, in the infiltration course, we were not sure whether Loren was joking. True, it was painful to crawl for hundreds of yards over rocks, with live machine gun fire above the barbed wire overhead. When Loren told us he was going to stand up and get it over with, Bob and I mustered all our powers of persuasion, honed by two years of selling door-to-door. "See those trees at the edge of the infiltration course," we said, "why don't you crawl over there, run away, and go AWOL? Better to spend a few years in Leavenworth than eternity dead." It must have worked, because Loren did finish the infiltration course, cursing the rocks, the barbed wire, the Army, and the "buddy plan."

At the end of each day during the final week of basic training, we all checked the company bulletin board to see if "orders" had been posted, announcing our "military occupational specialty" and next training station. What valuable training would I receive, I wondered: auto mechanics, radar repair, cook? I was pretty sure that I would not be assigned to the infantry. After all, what if every man in my squad were killed, and I had to pick up the radio? It was with ironic amusement, therefore, that I read my assignment: U.S. Army Southeastern Signal School. My military occupational specialty—radio teletype operator—a radio operator. So much for military intelligence!

Eight weeks of physical training, marching, and shooting transformed my buddies and me from pathetic door-to-door peddlers to lean, mean, fighting machines with "military bearing." Our boots were spit polished, our "gig lines" were straight, and we could tell an officer from a noncom. Salute the former; fear the latter.

But all good things must end; so it was with basic training. The Army gave us our first pay, in cash, and a ten-day leave before we were to report to our next training station. Before I could purchase my bus ticket to Chicago, someone broke into my wall locker and stole all of my money—$87.00. As my fellow soldiers hefted their duffle bags and boarded the Greyhound in their dress uniforms, I sat on the steps of the barracks, head in hands. A familiar voice asked what I was doing. Upon hearing my tale of woe, Sergeant Miller called to a group of G.I.s piling into a car. "Hey, y'all going to Chicago?" So I squeezed into the car and got home.

The next day, I walked to the Fifth Army Headquarters in Hyde Park, where the Red Cross had an office. The Red Cross made me a loan of $20, which I used to buy merchandise. Over the next week, I parlayed the money into bus fare to Ft. Gordon, Georgia, by selling door-to-door.

The U.S. Army Southeastern Signal School was certainly not like college; it consisted of classes in military radio procedure, operation of various kinds of equipment, construction of antennas, typing, and Morse Code. Typing turned out to be useful in civilian life, even though I still have to look at the keyboard to type numbers. Morse Code was the most important skill to master. If a trainee did not progress at the required pace, listening to code through headphones all afternoon, he had to come back after dinner. The instructor advised us to have a couple of beers before the evening session, "to relax you." The consequences of flunking out of radio teletype school were dire; you were sent to "pole climbing school." If you flunked out of that, you were shipped to the infantry. I was grateful that I would be able to talk on the radio without having to wait for all my buddies to be killed, so I studied hard and passed radio school.

Still, signal school was not as regimented as basic training had been. There were opportunities to get a pass on the weekend, so I visited Augusta. It was my first time in the South, and the experience proved to be quite a cultural shock. Segregation was still the law in Georgia. There were dual washrooms and drinking fountains; one set for "colored," and one for "white." Plumbers must have been happy.

In my part of Chicago, I had always felt mentally inferior to Jews and physically inferior to Negroes. That had seemed fair—a realistic appraisal of ability. The forced segregation of Blacks in the South did not make me feel superior to them. I felt greater kinship with the folks in the back of the bus than with the hillbilly driver. Once, I encountered an elderly Negro gentleman on a narrow footbridge over the Savannah River. He nearly bent backward over the railing, trying to make room for me. Respectful of his age, I moved aside for him and said, "Please sir, go ahead." He did, but with no sign of friendliness. Was he resentful that a young white punk could decide which local norms to ignore, but he couldn't? I think I would be.

Other encounters with the natives were simply amusing. Hiking on a country road one day, I came across a '56 Ford parked on the side of the road. A teenaged girl was sleeping in the back seat. Perhaps 1,000 yards beyond the car, two crackers, about my age, were walking toward the car. What's the proper greeting around here, I wondered. Then I remembered Hopalong Cassidy on television: "Howdy," I said. They passed me without a word.

A few moments later, I heard them running back toward me. "Give me your money!" one of them ordered.

Sizing them up, I replied that I wouldn't be walking along this God-forsaken road if I had any money.

The one who had not spoken previously belied his amateur status: "I don't need money this bad."

"Well I do," said the other guy, "show me your pockets!"

I felt like laughing, but I threw down my Brownie camera and snarled, "you want something, come get it!" Without another word, they turned and walked away.

I continued my hike, wondering what kind of place this was, where would-be robbers simply asked their victims for money. In Chicago, my head would have been bashed in and the two dollars removed from my shoe.

It was at Ft. Gordon, in July, that I saw a rebroadcast of a speech President Kennedy had made earlier that day. He was in Berlin, before a wildly cheering crown of Germans: *"...All free men are citizens of Berlin. Therefore, as a free man, I take pride in the words, Ich bin ein Berliner."*

The German face in the newsreel was not the face of a Gestapo agent slapping his hapless victim and shouting, *"Schweinhund!"* that I had seen in old war movies. It was not the face of a "Nazi," the synonym for "German" used by so many of my high school classmates, children of Holocaust victims. It was the face of a young boy, full of hope for the future and faith in the American commitment to his city.

When I completed signal school, my orders came down: Headquarters, 2nd Armored Cavalry, Nürnberg, Germany. During the ten-day voyage, I looked out to sea and fantasized about how I would serve my country in Germany. Little did I realize how much my experience in Germany would change the rest of my life—especially when I met Gerdi.

A tunnel under Nuremberg

CHAPTER THREE

Monk, My Mentor

So here I was, on Christmas Eve in Germany, in a pitch-black tunnel from the *SS Kaserne* to—where? Maybe this tunnel led to the *Zeppelinfeld*, a short distance away. I had heard that Hitler used such a tunnel to reach the stadium there, where his delirious supporters camped for days, waiting for their *Führer* to arrive. Another story circulated among the G.I.s was that, in 1945, SS troops were able to hold off the American 45th Infantry for two weeks by bringing supplies and reinforcements into the Kaserne through tunnels like this. Perhaps this tunnel even connected to the catacombs beneath the imperial castle in the walled old city, I thought. The fact that I was able to breathe assured me that air was flowing, so there must be an opening ahead. I rose to my feet, my panic and disorientation replaced with faith in God.

Following the wall with my right hand and waving my left hand in front of my face to deflect spider webs, I walked on for what seemed like hours. Finally, a light appeared ahead; I was saved! The light was streaming through cracks in a heavy plank wall. Peering through one of the cracks, I saw something salmon-colored, like the sandstone used in the oldest part of medieval Nürnberg. Had I really walked through a tunnel from the SS Kaserne, to the *Sebaldus* quarter of the old city, four miles north?

Elated at my discovery, I tugged at the boards with my bare hands. They wouldn't budge. I looked around in the dim light for something metal to use as a pry bar—perhaps a pipe or reinforcing rod used in construction of the tunnel. Half buried in the silt was a long pole. The shaft was hexagonal, and it had an inverted teardrop-shaped, pointed metal tip. It looked odd—sort of like the pikes displayed in the *Ger-*

manisches Nationalmuseum. I thought that it might have been stored here, along with other antiquities, during the air raids of World War II.

I had run across stranger storage places in my explorations of Nürnberg. One Sunday afternoon the previous summer, I had entered the courtyard of the half-donut shaped Congress Hall, rumored to have been built as the future headquarters of the National Socialist Party, with offices designated for Hitler, his henchmen, and leaders of the defeated nations: Stalin, Churchill, and Roosevelt. (Many stories circulated among the gullible G.I.s.) Spotting an open basement window, I had slithered in. Stairs led to a third floor office overlooking the *Dutzendteich,* an area of lakes, parkland, and the Nazi party rally grounds. An elaborate mural, depicting scenes from Teutonic mythology, flowed across one entire wall of the large room. I decided that this must have been intended as Hitler's office. For a few minutes, I imagined the evil little man standing there plotting the overthrow of some small country on the other side of the world in his quest for global hegemony. At that moment, I was proud to be part of a military deterrent to such aggressive ambition.

The next room in the apparently abandoned building was locked. I had to know what lay behind the opaque glass door, so I picked up a brick and made a hole large enough for my head. What I saw caused me to quickly withdraw my head and leave the building at a run: The entire room was stacked with brand-new bicycles in fresh cartons! The "abandoned room" was obviously being used as a warehouse, possibly patrolled by armed guards!

* * *

The pike did not work as a lever—the planks were too massive—but its metal point penetrated rotten spots in the wood. I was able to enlarge the cracks, little by little, until there was a man-sized hole. I crawled through—a shoeless eighteen-year-old American, blackened head to toe with tunnel soot. It occurred to me that the fine German *Bürgers,* on their way to Christmas mass at St. Sebaldus might be startled at the sight of me, but I didn't care.

I squeezed through the opening to face a bright new world. Sunlight glistened on new-fallen snow in this narrow alley running inside the old city wall. The tolling of Christmas bells announced that my long, dark night was over at last. I could return to the barracks and get some sleep, but I would have a lot of explaining to do. I did not have a pass; I had missed bed check, and I was a disgrace to my uniform—no boots or headgear, and my rumpled fatigues, caked with grease from the previous day's K.P., were blackened with silt from the tunnel. The guards at the front gate would assume that I had gone AWOL, gotten drunk, possibly laid, and probably rolled. It would be a reasonable assumption on their part. I would take whatever consequences awaited me when I presented myself to the unit police. Circumstances left no time for deliberation; the December wind was much colder than the tunnel had been, and I had not one *Pfnennig* in my pockets for taxi fare. I set off walking, in my stocking feet, toward the barracks, about four miles away, looking like an overdone gingerbread man.

This out-of-the-way corner of the old city seemed familiar, yet unfamiliar. I had often explored the crooked old streets near the *Burg*—the Imperial Castle presiding over the oldest part of the walled, inner city. It had always stirred my imagination, taking me five hundred years into the city's glorious past, when it was host to *diets* (meetings) of the Holy Roman Empire. Only when a Volkswagen putted by, or in one instance, the "dunt-da-DUNT-dunt" theme music from the "Dragnet" TV show reached my ears from an open window, did I return from my reverie to the 1960s.

The peal of bells from St. Sebaldus Church told me that I was headed in the right direction, but everything looked strange. There was no traffic, and no cars were parked on the street. Then I noticed that there was a gap between the paving stones and the fronts of some houses. Of course—the street must be closed for construction. Even the funny traffic signs, with their red circles, silhouetted figures, and triangles, and the utility lines were gone. The lack of twentieth century amenities accented the medieval feel of that crooked little street. When I came to the main street, there were people strolling toward *St. Sebaldus*—all dressed in period costumes of 16th century Nürnberg. I was sure that I had stumbled upon a movie set—a film producer taking advantage of the holiday to close the streets.

One of the men looked in my direction, his face contorted with fear. He shouted in a strange dialect, *"Außlander!"*

Catwalk inside city wall

Believing that I had angered him by stepping into a scene being filmed, I shrugged a gesture of "sorry" and backed away.

From somewhere out of sight came the shrill sound of a whistle, and eight men, dressed in period costumes and carrying pikes, approached me, their eyes wide with fear, as though they were stalking a wild animal. If they were acting, they were very good; if not, I was in trouble.

"*Hilfe!*" I shouted to them, thinking that if I called for help, they would realize that my otherworldly appearance was the result of distress rather than lunacy. They continued to advance on me, clearly determined to take me into custody—or worse. My instincts told me to run.

One of the men blocked the "rabbit hole" in the wall from whence I had entered this surreal world; clearly, these men were well trained and knew every inch of the territory. However, youthful speed and agility were on my side, as was a terror-induced adrenaline rush. The older, heavily clad men moved with a deliberateness born of duty and a sluggishness born of dread; I'm not sure that they really wanted to catch such an unpredictable, alien creature. Much to the surprise of the man crouched before my escape hole, I jumped on his back and, using it as a springboard, leapt to the catwalk above. The covered catwalk, wide enough for two fully armed sentries, was a great running track; I reached a bend in the wall, out of sight of my pursuers, before they climbed the stairs at the end of the alley. My head start allowed me to look for openings, but I saw none. It appeared that I was trapped.

The wall zigzagged, slowing my pace but blocking my assailants' view. I stopped for only a moment to look back, when something grabbed me. I felt myself being pulled through an opening in the wall! My butt hit the floor of a tiny space, perhaps six feet by twelve feet. In the semi-darkness, I saw the back of a robed figure pushing shut the heavy door through which I had entered the chamber. Sounds of running footsteps on the wooden catwalk grew louder and then faded away.

My rescuer, an old man, turned to face me, an expression of alert tranquility on his bearded face. His brown, hooded robe, tied with a length of coarse rope, reminded me of the little monk depicted on bottles of beer brewed in Munich (*München*, or "little monk"). His finger to his lips warned me to be still until the citizen posse was safely past. He need not have worried; I was struck dumb by my circumstances, as one's frustrating inability to speak in a dream.

For the first time since I had emerged from the tunnel, I considered my predicament. I had apparently stumbled upon a reenactment of some historic event. Had I spoiled the filming of a movie, as I had first supposed, or was this some kind of pageant? Whatever the case, those guys chasing me were not acting; they were really angry. This fellow in the monk's getup had gone out of his way to help.

"Thanks, buddy," I said, "You saved me from a heap of trouble."

His response was calm silence. I switched to my G.I. German: *"Danke schön, mein Freund."* I could probably get through to him with a combination of simple German phrases and nonverbal signs, I thought. I had often experienced that level of communication in German pubs, for beer was a great social lubricant.

Once, a redneck G.I. buddy, after a few beers with the guy next to him in a German bar, expressed his opinion of the late *Führer:* "The hell with Hitler!" His German drinking companion misunderstood Sgt. Jackson's accent and meaning, with happy results: *"Heil Hitler!"* he responded. The G.I. and the German continued to drink lustfully, toasting each other with "Hell with Hitler!" and *"Heil Hitler!"* until patrons around them showed signs of restlessness, and I put Sgt. Jackson into a cab.

The monk character did not say anything in response to my thanks, so I tried again, asking in pigeon German what was going on. He motioned for me to sit on a crude wooden bench and poured some white wine into a ceramic mug. It was delicious. I relaxed for the first time since the ruckus started in the barracks last night. Was it only last night? It seemed like a different world—my escape from the gang of drunken G.I.s, the long, black night in the tunnel, my emergence into this weird place and escape from the angry citizen posse, and now this den inside the city wall of Nürnberg and the old guy dressed as a monk. The adrenalin that fueled my flight after fourteen hours of K.P. dissipated with the wine and the warm blanket my new friend placed around my shoulders. I sagged onto the bench and fell into a sound sleep.

When I opened my eyes, it was dark. Had I slept through Christmas Day, 1965? Where was Mom? Where were the presents? The tree? The turkey dinner? Oh, I'm in the Army, I remembered—in Germany. But this wasn't my room in the barracks! Then the events of the previous night returned with a rush. Fully awake now, I scanned my hole in the wall. A single candle flame illuminated the face of the monk. When he saw me stirring, he came closer.

"*Guten Abend*," I said, "good evening."

Good morning, Bob," he replied, in an unmistakable Chicago accent, "it's close to dawn. And yes, you did sleep through Christmas Day—and night." So much for this guy's vow of silence! And how did he know my name?

"You're American!"

"Well, sort of," he said, "It's rather complicated. We'll get to all that, but how about some breakfast?"

Without another word, the monk turned and stoked a small fire to heat water. By the time breakfast—an earthy tasting tea and black bread—was served, the window revealed a pale dawn. I took a few steps to the tiny window, about four feet above the floor and noted, with shock, that there was nothing but snow-covered fields and forests beyond the wall. Having circumnavigated the city wall on several occasions in my solitary explorations of Nürnberg, I knew that modern commercial, industrial, and residential development surrounded the old city in every direction. The fog that had enveloped me, the disorientation, returned. Where was I? Who were these weird people? Was this all a dream?

The monk saw the panic in my eyes. He urged me to eat and drink.

This I did with relish, not having eaten since the day before. The monk joined me, but he approached the meal as if it were a sacrament, savoring each bite. His attire and manner suggested that he was, indeed, a member of some religious order.

When we finished our simple meal, I surveyed the little cell, now bathed in morning light. The front and back walls were rough sandstone, being defined by the outer and inner dimensions of the city wall. The door through which I had entered this chamber led to the wooden, second-floor catwalk on the city side of the wall. The lone "window" opening may have been a port through which *Nürnbergers* could defend the city from attack. I surmised that ramparts were above the plaster ceiling, and the floor was, as I mentioned earlier, wood. The only other architectural feature was a small fireplace, on which were hung a few simple cooking utensils, like something out of the Old West. Furniture consisted of a rough wooden table and a couple of benches of similar construction. Oh yes, there was a shelf as well, with what appeared to be three or four antique books.

Still seated at the table, I tried again to communicate with the monk: "So what's going on? Is this a movie set, a recreation of medieval Nürnberg outside of town? Are you an Army shrink, conducting some kind of psychological experiment on me?"

"I'll tell you everything you want to know—and a lot more—in due time, Bob, but we have to take it slow. You have been through a traumatic experience and a drastic transformation."

"A transformation? What are you talking about? And how do you know my name, by the way?"

The monk sat on the other bench, facing me across the table. "The adrenaline pumping through your system enabled you to flee from danger back in the Army barracks on Christmas Eve, 1965 Anno Domini."

"Anno Domini?"

"A.D."

"Oh."

"At some point during your long, black night of soul searching, that chemical acted as a catalyst for the melding of your conscious mind and personal unconscious with the *Collective Unconscious* of all humanity."

"Collective unconscious?"

"Yes. A psychologist named Carl Jung first proposed that term in the early part of your century."

"My century?"

"The twentieth century Anno Domini. Anyway, the idea is that we are all connected with everyone who has ever lived by our collective human experiences and memories."

I had heard of Carl Jung and his theory of the Collective Unconscious. Actually, I was quite interested in psychology and spent many hours in the tiny base library, searching for "serious" reading among the racks of detective stories, westerns, and military manuals that comprised the bulk of its "literature." I usually had the entire library to myself, as most G.I.s were in the Enlisted Men's Club, the PX, or the base theater when they were not on duty. (Passes to go off base, or "hit the strasse," in G.I. parlance, were often restricted because of incidents between soldiers and civilians.)

I had once discovered Sigmund Freud's *The Interpretation of Dreams* in the library and sat down to peruse it when the alert buzzer sounded.

During the Cold War, all NATO forces were required to respond to a monthly alert with no prior notice. When the alert sounded, everyone grabbed their weapons and gear and took up combat-ready positions in the field. Tensions with the Soviets were such that we never knew whether we were responding to a monthly drill or the real thing.

When the alert buzzer sounded that day, I ran out of the base library and found the members of my unit forming into ranks in the quadrangle outside our quarters. I fell into the formation and stood at attention as the platoon sergeant strode between the rows, giving instructions and inspecting each soldier. When he came to me, he bellowed, "What's that?"

In my haste, I had run out of the library with the book still in my hand. "A *book*, Sergeant!" (I harbored a haughty eighteen-year-old's disdain for Army "lifers.")

Sergeant Holmes did not appreciate the irony. He read the title, *The Interpretation of Dreams* and declaimed his opinion of such reading material: "WHAT ARE YOU, SOME KIND OF FAGGOT?"

"No Sergeant!" I had barked, my face burning.

* * *

Now, this gentle man in monk's garb was speaking of Carl Jung's Collective Unconscious as though it was more than a theory, as though it was a reality—my reality.

"Can you explain?" I asked.

"Yes, Bob, I shall try to make this as comfortable for you as possible, but you must steel yourself for a revelation beyond anything you have ever experienced."

* * *

"First, Bob, I know your name because I know everything about you."

"Oh, just as I suspected; you're from G-2."

"No, I am not from military intelligence, Bob, I represent a higher intelligence."

"CIA?"

"Higher."

"Higher than CIA? I don't believe it! No one from the White House would be interested in a twenty-year-old Sp/4. I'm not even airborne qualified."

"I'm not from the government at all, Bob, and I do care about you. In fact, you are the center of my life."

"Well buddy, you must be my *Doppelganger*," I joked, "because no one else cares more about me than I do."

"Exactly. I am you—that spirit within you that connects you to God and to all of humanity through the Collective Unconscious."

"I get it now; I must have conked my head in that tunnel, and I'm in a coma. You are a delusion."

"The biochemical process that brought us together is a reality," admitted the monk, "but only one reality. More importantly, you are here—really here."

"Where's here?"

"You are in sixteenth century Nürnberg, a place you have often imagined as you walked these crooked little streets while on leave from Merrill Barracks."

The sense of panic that had gripped me ever since my arrival in this eerie place evaporated in my supposition that this was all a dream, albeit an extremely realistic one. I decided to make the most of this lucid dream, this unconscious adventure. "That explains the lack of cars and utility poles and the view from this room—just fields and forests."

"Yes."

"And now, I suppose," I said to the monk, "you are going to give me a tour of sixteenth century Nürnberg, the great imperial city of the Holy Roman Empire."

"I shall, indeed, be your guide and mentor, Bob, but the real journey will be within your own psyche, for you must meet and conquer your own dragons before you return to the life you knew."

"Ah yes, an odyssey," I responded, feeling a bit cocky in my ability to take charge of my "dream."

"Yes—an odyssey that will determine the kind of man you become." The monk's eyes and voice were gentle, yet powerful, like those of the Reverend Martin Luther King, Jr., whom I had met in a little Baptist church on the South Side of Chicago five years earlier. His conviction and sincerity, as he spoke these words, humbled me and carried a message: I would have to prove myself through my own actions, in this journey, but I was not in charge of the monk.

"Brother," I said, overcome with sudden humility, "lead me; I am ready."

The monk smiled for the first time and opened his arms in a warm embrace. I distinctly remember how good it felt, even in a dream, to entrust my future to that spiritual power, so full of wisdom and love for me. For the first time in my life, I did not feel alone.

"Let us begin this journey with a clear view of its destination, Bob. I want you to tell me about your life as you envisioned it as a nine-year-old boy, lying on your hideaway bed in the front room of that shabby little house on Ridgeland Avenue. What was your image of a man?"

I recalled the exact scene the monk was describing: the hot, summer night; the still life painting hung on the wall—a bowl of roses, each of which I had assigned a unique face and personality.

"I was staring up at the painting of roses over my bed. One of the roses, the one I called 'Rosie,' seemed to speak to me, asking me when I would be a man. I had conversations with those roses all the time—active imagination, I guess."

"I remember," said the monk.

"He remembers?" I thought, "Had the monk really been there? Was he the 'imaginary friend' who accompanied me on my childhood explorations of my home, my block, and the surrounding neighborhoods? Was he the sounding board of my mental explorations, my conscience, and the one I had assumed to be Jesus?"

"I believe that I answered the rose's question in terms of chronology. At the time, I thought that perhaps at twenty-five years of age I would be a man."

"So you thought that you would automatically become a man at the age of twenty-five. Did you consider what sort of man you would be?"

"Well, no—not really. I mean, I guess I thought I would be pretty much the same as I was then, just bigger."

"Did you have a role model—a man you wished to emulate?"

"Not my dad, that's for sure!"

"Do you remember where your dad was that night?"

"Yes—in his boxer shorts, pacing between the kitchen at the rear of the four-room shack and the "comic book case," an upright walnut-stained chest with a flimsy curtain across the front. He would take a sip of wine from his tumbler on top of the comic book case and pace back to the kitchen, perhaps for some peanuts. He did not pay much attention to the twelve-inch black and white television in the "front room" that night; there was no boxing match or ball game on. I had no idea what he was thinking about. He didn't talk."

"Why do you suppose he didn't talk that evening?"

"I don't recall his ever talking to us—carrying on a regular conversation. When he did speak, it was usually to bark an order, followed by the command, 'Mind!' and a swat to my head. I got pretty good at ducking."

"Wasn't this lack of communication with your father difficult?"

"His silence was far preferable to the fights. He and my mother would go at it for hours, screaming terrible, cruel accusations and threats to each other. Those bouts would usually end with my dad walking out and my mother continuing her harangue, with us as her audience: 'I put him in jail once, and I'll do it again!'"

"How do you think that growing up in such an environment affected you?"

"It taught me to avoid conflict, to walk away from it, as I saw my father do, and to keep to myself."

"And yet, as I recall, you were no stranger to conflict."

"I did get into a lot of fights…"

"How?"

"Well, you know how boys are; they gotta know if they can 'take' you."

"The pecking order, right?"

"Yeah—any excuse to start a fight."

"Like being different? Avoiding the conflict of competitive sports? Not swearing, that sort of thing?"

"You got it, Brother; they used to require each guy to say a cuss word in order to take part in their little adventures."

"And you would walk away, rather than violate your mother's rule about not swearing?"

"You make it sound like I was a mama's boy."

"Not at all, Bob; you simply valued your own sense of morality more than the companionship of other kids."

"Well, they were constantly arguing about what we would do, who was in charge—all that stuff—and I had enough arguing at home."

"But as a result of your attempt to avoid conflict by being a loner, you got into fights."

"I had no choice. They would start it, and I would finish it. Most of the time, I won."

"Did that make you feel pretty good?"

"Not really; I would usually run home afterward, sobbing."

"Because of the pain?"

"Naw, like I said, I usually won. In fact, the more I won, the more I got challenged. All that practice made me pretty tough."

"But by the time you got home, you were sobbing."

"Yeah, I just hated to fight."

"So you withdrew."

"Yep, as long as I stayed away from other people, I had no problem."

"So Bob, we're talking about manhood here. How do you think this strategy of avoiding people is going to enable you to become the kind of man you want to be?"

"I guess I'm going to have to learn to deal with people."

"And conflict."

"And conflict."

"We are going to work on that, Bob. You and I are here, in sixteenth century Nürnberg, for a reason. You are going to meet some people who are going to introduce you to the potential of your own soul."

"To deal with conflict?"

"That is part of it. There is more, but we will take one step at a time."

"You're going to make a man out of me?"

"No, Bob, you are going on this journey yourself. There is no guarantee; in fact, there is a very real possibility that you will not return."

"Why here? Why now?"

"It gets complicated—has to do with genetics, the *Butterfly Effect*—changes that would upset too many people if they came too close to your birth lifetime. Besides, the right people and the right circumstances are here and now."

"Won't my mom miss me if I don't return from this odyssey?"

"It will be as if you never existed."

"You've got my attention, Brother; what do I have to do?"

"First, some ground rules. You are going to have to survive. You got a taste of the reception these folks will give you if they discover that you are an alien. You know nothing of their worldview, culture, or social customs.

"I get your point," I said, remembering the fear and hatred in the eyes of those men when they spotted me in my Army fatigues.

"You don't speak their language."

"I know some German," I protested, *"Was ist los, Comrade?"*

"I rest my case; you don't speak their language. In 1965, you were barely able to order a beer in the *Gasthaus.*"

"Okay, so I'll bone up on my German."

"It is not quite that easy, Bob. The German language changed as much as English from the sixteenth to the twentieth century. Do you talk like Shakespeare?"

"No."

"Exactly—so listen carefully. We talked about the Collective Unconscious and how you are connected to the collective memory of all humanity, right?"

"Right."

"You have made an extraordinary leap to a place and time in the Collective Unconscious, but it is going to take awhile to access the data in that memory. You will pick up the language fast, first listening, then speaking. In the meantime, I have a plan for you to get out of here and find your way around the city."

CHAPTER FOUR

The Hangman

C loaked in vestments borrowed from the friendly "Monk," my alien
tongue muted by His vow of silence, I walked freely among the
Bürgers of sixteenth century Nürnberg. They greeted one another
warmly and went about their business with creative energy—proud, uni-
fied citizens of a great imperial city.

My initial impression contrasted sharply with generally held notions of city life during that period. Like most people, I had imagined muddy streets strewn with filth and general chaos—a scene from
Great Expectations. Here, however, the streets were paved with cobble-
stones, in good repair. Some were slightly curved, so that the buildings
fronting them were slightly offset from one another. Thus, the front
part of each building was exposed on one side, allowing the occupants to have windows for light and fresh air. The narrow, four and
five story buildings had room for only a few windows on the street
side. Space within the walled city was at a premium, I reasoned, much
as in Chicago, so buildings went upward, rather than outward. As on
79th Street, in my old neighborhood, the street level of most buildings appeared to be dedicated to commerce: butcher shops, bakeries,
and artisans of all kinds, while the upper stories were apartments. I
did not recall, from my twentieth-century explorations of the old city
of Nürnberg, cisterns now in the middle of the street. These sources
of water must have been essential in the days before modern plumb-
ing. As I continued strolling through the city, the sight and smell of
compost heaps and pigs being herded to the Pegnitz River for a drink
revised my initial impression slightly and jolted my senses back to
reality. This was not some "fairy castle land," but a working city, where

people do not necessarily share my twentieth century notions of sanitation—or for that matter, "reality."

I was amazed and delighted that, alien as I was to the scene before me, it was vaguely familiar. The general configuration of Nürnberg—a rhomboid divided by the Pegnitz River into the older, *St. Sebaldus* parish, with its imposing castle on a hill overlooking the city, and the *St. Lorenz* parish to the south—the two halves united by a mighty wall, with numerous towers and fortified gates, was sufficiently like the post-World War II Nürnberg I had known so that I could walk from one landmark to another confident that I would not get lost. I contemplated circumnavigating the entire wall (about four and a half miles), as I had often done as a G.I., but that would be more complicated in this era before sidewalks. After my initial meandering from the oldest part of the city, where Monk had rescued me, I found myself at an impressive tower and entrance to the walled city at the southeast corner of town. As a G.I., I had known this as the *Königstor,* or King's Tower. I would usually begin my exploration of the old city from this point after walking two miles, or so, from the main gate of Merrill Barracks, the American name for the *SS Kaserne.* A broad commercial street, called *Königstraße,* or King's Street, lead to the Imperial Castle. Now, following a familiar route would help me to get my bearings.

The first thing I noticed was that the sixteenth-century *Frauentor* (as the Königstor was then called, I was to learn) was much more of a fortification than I remembered. The 1965 Königstor had been a sort of archway, a welcoming portal to the walled city, through which vehicles and pedestrians passed. The city gate I now encountered felt more like a trap. From my vantage point in a sort of walled courtyard, I looked south. There were fields, a few farmhouses, and a strange apparatus on the spot later occupied by the main train station, where I had first arrived in Nürnberg after ten days at sea and an overnight rail trip from Bremerhaven. My addled brain perceived something dangling from the apparatus—could it be a human form? I shook my head to clear the image, much as one might do upon waking from an unpleasant dream. Directly before me was a moat, maybe 100 feet wide, surrounding the city walls. People approaching Nürnberg from the south would cross the moat on a sturdy bridge. A guardhouse controlled traffic from that direction. Between the guardhouse and the city was a drawbridge that could be raised in time of siege to fit into an opening in the wall. On this sunny winter day, people streamed across the bridge and through the courtyard in which I stood. I followed the crowd, trying to blend in. Inside the outer wall, the path angled to slow unwelcome visitors. Enemy troops who made it to the open space between inner and outer walls would have been sitting ducks for arrows or other missiles that the defenders of the city would rain upon them. I scurried through the open doors of the Frauentor, intimidated by the drop gates overhead, even though I posed no threat in my "monk's" cassock.

No sign marked the street I had known as *Königstraße*, but it had a familiar feel. I immediately recognized the huge *Kornhaus*, with its steep roof, covered with dozens of gabled windows for drying six stories of grain. I had once passed a couple of hours in the beer cellar of that building with a Greek guest worker. The man had expressed wonder at the rather reserved manner of the German crowd, compared to the volubility of a similar gathering of his compatriots. Now, peering from under my brown hood at teams of horses pulling carts loaded with grain into the newly completed Kornhaus, an eerie sensation compelled me to move on. Continuing north, the street became narrower. I recall reading an explanation: I was now entering the oldest part of the city, inside what had once been an earlier ring of walls.

Looming on my right was the large parish church of *St. Lorenz*, for which this half of the city is named. I pulled open one of the heavy front doors under a stained-glass rosette window, perhaps twenty feet in diameter, and entered the church. My head was spinning; I needed to sit quietly and meditate. Amid the splendor of this sanctuary, perhaps I could understand the mystical experience that brought me here. Biblical scenes of creation, tales from the Old Testament, the birth, life, and death of Christ were revealed in stain glass, paintings, and statuary. My gaze fell upon a resplendent *Annunciation*—the angel Gabriel's announcement to Mary that she was to give birth to Jesus. How did Mary feel, I wondered, when she learned that she was to be thrust in a role that would change the world? I recalled, from Sunday School, that "she kept these things in her heart." Apparently, she did not freak out; she kept her cool and carried out God's will. Surely, I too could fulfill the mission assigned to me by Monk, whatever that mission might be. Over time, light passing through the stained glass windows of St. Lorenz painted its pink sandstone wall with rosy warmth. My panic subsided. My need to be in control of my destiny faded. Knowing not where I was going, I yielded to Fate and to God. *"Have Thine own way Lord; Thou hast put me here, in this time and place for a reason that Thou wilt reveal in due time."*

Leaving St. Lorenz, I continued walking north, across the *Museumsbrücke.* To my right, under an external skeleton of wooden rigging, was the Holy Ghost Hospital. I recalled the first time I had laid eyes on the *Heiliggeist-Spital* in 1963, spanning the *Pegnitz* River in two graceful arches, and marveled at the humanity of a people who would provide such a beautiful setting for their sick and dying. Ahead, I knew, would be the main market place—the *Hauptmarkt.*

The Hauptmarkt was at once familiar and strange. It was, even in the sixteenth century, a large, open space at the convergence of streets from north, east, south, and west. The Beautiful Fountain, or Schönen Brunnen, marked the northwest corner of the market place, and the Ladies' Church, or Frauenkirche, anchored it to the east. The market place teamed with activity, just as it had in my own time, but it had a very different feel. In contrast to the Hauptmarkt of my twentieth-century memory, with its flower vendors and souvenir stands, I saw the highest quality goods of Nürnberg's best artisans. Fascinated, I wandered among the carts and stalls, insulated by my monk's cassock, but listening to the babble of vendors and shoppers. It was a strange version of German, almost like Yiddish. Presently, my ears became attuned to certain words: the names of articles being discussed—an ebony compass case, a comb made of genuine bullhorn, a flintlock rifle, for example. When buyers and sellers haggled, I picked up the words for numbers. An officious-looking gentleman, possibly a public inspector, made clear, with his nonverbal cues, such words as "quality" and "inferior." He seemed displeased with one piece of pewter and destroyed it on the spot, providing no compensation to the vendor. Greetings and salutations were obvious; that was understandable. However, I was baffled at the ease with which I seemed to be picking up sixteenth-century German words. Did this phenomenon have something to do with Monk's explanation? Was my experience of this time and place really a voyage to the Collective Unconscious of Mankind? If so, that might explain my swift facility with a foreign tongue as spoken hundreds of years before my own time.

I passed an hour or so in the market place, observing the manners and mores of the people, along with the exquisitely crafted products of the city's artisans. Suddenly, a commotion stirred me from my reverie:

"*Dibio!*" cried a red-faced merchant, pointing to an old woman, scurrying away from his cart, "Thief!" She then attempted to flee from the market place, but a group of bystanders seized her. The merchant plunged his hand into her basket and held up a small blanket, which he claimed she had stolen from his cart. The terrified face of the old woman did not look like that of a thief. Leaving his cart in the hands of an assistant, the merchant and his ad hoc posse dragged the woman and the evidence from the market. They proceeded to the City Hall, or *Rathaus,* adjacent to the Hauptmarkt. Among the small group of curious spectators following the procession that cold, December day was a young woman clutching a tiny baby inside her threadbare dress. The make-believe "monk" brought up the rear.

Inside the Rathaus, a grave gentleman, richly attired in cape, collar, and breeches, received the accuser, accused, and the entire agitated group in a special hall. The mood was between that of a courtroom and a lynching. The official, apparently some sort of magistrate, addressed the merchant. "Who prosecutes this wretched soul?"

The merchant, out of his marketplace milieu, no longer cart commander, hawker, huer and crier, assumed a demeanor appropriate to the gravity of his august surroundings. "I, Herr Gräber, your honor."

"On what offense, Herr Gräber?

"Your honor, this creature stole a fine, wool blanket from my cart on the marketplace."

Turning to the old woman, now trembling with fear, the magistrate demanded, "And what say you, woman?"

The poor woman stammered, "No your honor, I am no thief."

"Your name, woman, your name!" roared the magistrate.

The woman mumbled something, then repeated her name: "Frau Merk, your honor, of Nürnberg.

The magistrate then looked over the people assembled before him. His gaze fell upon me for a brief moment—the first time I had been scrutinized since assuming my monastic garb. I did my best not to tremble. This official, despite his foppish appearance, clearly held power over life and death. He then asked if any of those present had witnessed the alleged crime. Six men from among those who had accosted the old woman stepped forward. The magistrate interrogated them as to their names, citizenship, and occupation. Apparently satisfied that they were respectable citizens, he asked for their account of the incident. They unanimously corroborated Herr Gräber's story.

Only the sound of a hungry baby's cry could be heard as the magistrate prepared to speak. When he did, the meaning of his words eluded my emerging understanding of sixteenth-century German: "Fetch the *Lion*!"

All but the "monk" reacted instantly to the title, "*Lion*." The merchant snorted; his supporters murmured; some in the crowd gasped; the young mother wailed. I intuited a relationship between the old woman, accused of stealing a small blanket from the pushcart, and the young mom holding that wailing, precious bundle to her breast. At the same time, I surmised that the magistrate's call for the "*Lion*" was not a welcome development for the defendant, who now dropped to her knees.

"Please, your honor," she begged, "spare me! I swear to the Almighty that I only took the blanket to do His work, to give it to one of His tiny souls, that the baby may live."

The hall grew silent again. The magistrate regarded the pitiful old woman. Then he ordered her to her feet. "Take the blanket," he said. Her face regained a blush of color; the merchant, still holding his merchandise, furrowed his brow and pursed his lips. I felt that I was witnessing the wisdom of Solomon, the compassion of Jesus.

The accused walked uncertainly toward Herr Gräber, who looked down his nose at her and clutched the little blanket even tighter.

"Take it!" repeated the magistrate.

Frau Merk stretched out her left arm, trying to stay as far away from the merchant as possible. She grasped the blanket from the man's reluctant hand and returned to the magistrate.

"Put the blanket down!" said the magistrate.

She did.

"Hold the blanket up for all to see!" said the magistrate.

She did.

"Her left hand!" bellowed the magistrate. "Off with her left hand!" Once again, the spectators gasped, but their reaction was milder than when the judge summoned the Lion, and the prisoner appeared relieved that she had not been condemned to die. "Now take this woman to the *Loch,* where she will await the *Lion!*"

A bailiff, looking even more clownish than the patrician magistrate, in puffy blouse and pantaloons and a feathered, broad-brimmed hat, took charge of the prisoner. His sword and no-nonsense manner commanded respect, however. The magistrate left the hall, as did Herr Gräber and his friends. Based on the snatches of their conversation I heard, they were headed to a pub to celebrate their triumph. Only the young mother, her baby, and I remained in the room—along with the tiny blanket that lay where Frau Merk had dropped it when her sentence was pronounced. I handed it to the mom and hurried after the bailiff and his charge.

Relating this story to you now, Alex, I can understand your incredulity. How could I have been an ordinary G.I., pulling K.P. duty one day in 1965, and then, a couple days later, a fake "monk," following a condemned thief and her peacock-looking bailiff to a jail cell beneath the sixteenth-century Nürnberg city hall? I'm not sure that I understand myself, Alex, but bear with me; it gets even more interesting.

The bailiff paid no heed to me. Perhaps it was normal for clergy to minister to the poor souls in the *Loch,* or hole, in the bowels of the city. We entered a dark maze of stone cells—a dozen or more. Fumes of burning charcoal made me dizzy. The stench of human excrement was nauseating. Shadowy forms darted across the floor of the passage, which was illuminated only by an occasional oil lamp. At one such location, the sight of creepy, crawly, critters made me grateful for the general darkness. Finally, the bailiff stopped, opened a heavy, wooden door painted with the numeral eight. I was not allowed to enter the cell with the woman, but the colorfully dressed bailiff permitted me to remain in the Loch when he returned to the Rathaus above. It was impossible to converse normally with the prisoner, as the door to her cell had no openings, but I could make out what sounded like prayer coming from within. I rapped on her door and shouted, "God bless you, grandmother" using my newly acquired gift of language. The muffled sound of her voice stopped momentarily, then commenced again. Carefully I made my way along the corridor, observing that other doors were painted with symbols: a fiery red rooster, a black cat, and numerals six, seven, and eight. Perhaps these symbols were references to the occupants' offenses—arson, witchcraft. Perhaps the numeral referred to Biblical commandments, rather than cell numbers. The "eight" on Grandma's cell might signify the Eighth Commandment—"Thou shalt not steal."

I had little time to reflect on this theory or on the logic of granting clergy access to the Loch, but not to the prisoners therein, who may benefit from counseling, before the bailiff returned, accompanied by the Lion. The Lion was not a jungle beast, but a rather large, fearsome creature nonetheless. In contrast to the bailiff's fancy costume, the Lion was dressed in coarse clothing. Apparently, his purpose was to transport Grandma to the place where her sentence would be carried out. Grandma's cell was opened, and she rose from a rough bench to follow the bailiff and the Lion. I fell in behind the trio.

I was so relieved to exit the dank, foul-smelling Loch that I almost forgot the gruesome purpose of our short trek from the Rathaus. We walked along the edge of the Hauptmarkt, picking up a small escort of morbidly curious residents, and crossed a wooden bridge to an island in the Pegnitz. On the far end of this island, we came to a little house on a stone, arched bridge. I recognized it as the picturesque *Henkersteg*, or hanging bridge, in twentieth-century Nürnberg city guidebooks. This was, I recalled, home of the *Scharfrichter*, the Nürnberg hangman. Upon our arrival, the Scharfrichter appeared at the door of his little house. Like the Lion, his assistant (as I learned), the Scharfrichter was a big man. His appearance was, ironically, less fearsome than his assistant; he looked for all the world like a gentleman farmer. His clothing was neither coarse nor fine; his beard was full. His eyes were more like those of a scholar than those of a killer. He spoke privately with the Lion for a few minutes, pausing several times to look up at me. On one of these occasions, I inadvertently made eye contact with him, something I had avoided assiduously since assuming my role as the gentle, silent, "monk." When our eyes met, there was a human connection, a feeling that we had met somewhere, once upon a time.

The Scharfrichter got right to work. He walked directly to the large stone slab where his assistant, the Lion, had forced the old woman to kneel, her left hand stretched before her. She prayed feverishly, invoking God's blessing on her family and asking for courage. The onlook-

The Nuremberg hangman's house

ers talked among themselves, possibly discussing the sudden change of weather. Large snowflakes had begun to fall, turning the little courtyard white. The young woman from the marketplace nursed her baby, now a bulkier bundle under her dress. The child suckled blissfully, unaware of the sacrifice her grandmother was about to make for her. The Scharfrichter bound the old woman's arm above the wrist with strips of cloth and a stick from his woodpile. The Lion knelt beside the woman, pulling her against the side of his own body with one arm and restraining her outstretched arm with his other hand. The Scharfrichter removed a heavy sword from its scabbard at his waist, and with one stroke, the snow turned red.

The Lion released his grip on the old woman. He held up the severed hand for all to see. "This is the punishment for theft in the Imperial City of Nürnberg," he roared. An old man in peasant's garb came forward and offered to purchase the member. After some brief haggling, a deal was struck; money (and hand) changed hands.

Meanwhile, the Scharfrichter and the old lady's daughter had gone to her aid, applying pressure with the tourniquet and bandaging the wound. She was given a strong draught to ease the pain. I went to her and whispered, "I'm sorry" in English. Despite her agony, she looked into my eyes with understanding. Grandma, daughter, and baby left the scene. I looked after them, wondering if we would meet again. The crowd dissipated. The Lion cleaned up. The Scharfrichter sat on a wooden bench outside his cottage, looking pensive.

What was I to do now? If this horrible incident, this entire experience, was a dream, a journey into some collective intelligence stored in the universe, why did I, or Fate, choose to access it? Why did God lead me to the Scharfrichter, darkest symbol of the Dark Ages? What would this monster and his fearsome assistant do to me when they discovered my real identity? I sat down next to the Scharfrichter.

Time passed, and the Lion left to patrol the marketplace. The "monster" and the "monk" meditated. The stillness assuaged my fight-or-flight symptoms. "Have Thine own way, Lord, have Thine own way…"

Finally, the Scharfrichter spoke: "So, you have come, my friend."

"Friend?" I thought, I am this guy's friend? Was he expecting me?

As though he had read my mind, the Scharfrichter said, "I have been waiting for you, Bob."

Here we go again, I thought, like Monk, this man apparently knows all about me.

"Not really," said the Scharfrichter, "only about a certain part of you."

"Okay, so this guy is a mind reader," I thought, "nothing should surprise me anymore."

"And what part of me is that, Mr. Scharfrichter, or should I call you 'The Hangman' for short?"

His penetrating gaze and his answer, after a protracted pause, terrified me: "I am that part of you that you most fear, Bob; I am the *Warrior*."

"Warrior?" Remembering that I had stumbled into this weird place dressed in my G.I. fatigues, I responded as I would have to a member of the German Bundeswehr in the *Kaffeebohne* café: "*Kamerade!* I am a warrior too—a member of the United States Army."

The Scharfrichter smiled. "You donned the uniform of a soldier, Bob; you trained with the M1 rifle, bivouacked, and played war games. You are a G.I., but you are not yet a warrior."

"It's not my fault that the Ruskies haven't come across the border yet. That's why they call it the 'Cold War.'"

"Warriors may be born in combat, but they are most often developed in ordinary conflict situations as a boy becomes a man. How do you deal with conflict, Bob?"

I thought about the long walks I took, as a child, to escape the battles between my mom and dad. I thought about how I had avoided other kids because they were constantly competing for top rung on the pecking order. I thought about how I had run away from the drunken G.I.s who attacked a Commo guy outside my squad room on Christmas Eve. "I guess I would rather take flight than fight," I said.

"I have noticed," said the Scharflichter, rising to his feet, "but you must learn to stand and fight. Listen to me! I am the Warrior!"

I was still not clear how this "evil man" could teach me anything about becoming a man, but I was not about to ruffle his feathers. "Okay, okay!" I said, "I'll listen to you. Tell me what to do."

"The first thing you will do," replied the Scharflichter testily, is not to expect me, or anyone else, to spoon-feed you. Life is not your kindergarten teacher; it is your university classmate, competing in an exam graded on the curve. Life is your colleague at work, competing for the next promotion. Life is the force of evil, plotting to harm you and your loved ones. You must learn to be a warrior by taking the initiative, by developing a strategy, by asking direct questions."

"What am I supposed to learn?"

"You must learn to fight for right."

"But my mom told me it's not nice to fight."

"You must learn that 'nice' is not always right."

"But my mom always said, 'If you can't say anything nice, don't say anything at all.'"

"Your mother's job was to cage your Warrior, Bob; my job—and yours—is to release Him. You can only do that by asking the right questions." He sat down, a picture of patient expectation.

My purpose in being here—to encounter the Warrior—was clear. The task before me now was to ask the right questions—and to listen. But I had not prepared. What would I ask? Where would I begin? Monk's words stilled my anxiety: "This is the time, Bob; this is the place. You are ready." I drew a deep breath and began the interview.

"Herr Scharfrichter, Warrior, what are your values?"

"Duty, honor, and courage."

"Does your job as hangman compromise your moral values?"

"No, for I am the Warrior."

"When does the Warrior in you show?"

"When I do my duty, honorably and courageously."

"Do you like what you do?"

"No."

"Why do you do what you do?"

"It is my duty."

"How did you get this responsibility?"

"My father, and his father before him, practiced the trade. It was expected of me."

"Would you ever give up your job?"

"When I become too old to behead a man with a single, swift stroke of my ax, I shall turn my duties over to the Lion and become, once more, a respectable citizen."

"Is it hard coping with what your family, friends, and other people think about what you do?"

"Yes."

"How do you deal with it?"

"I never forget that, by enforcing the law, I am helping to give them a civilized, safe city. I perform my onerous duties out of love for all the citizens of Nürnberg."

"Did you ever try to help someone escape?"

"My sense of duty and honor would not allow that. The Council determines the fate of wrongdoers. I only execute the Council's decisions."

"Have you ever executed an innocent person?"

"The Council determines guilt or innocence. My duty is simply to carry out the sentence."

"Have you ever had to kill a family member?"

The Scharfrichter's voice cracked a little. "Unfortunately, yes. My own dear brother was condemned to be broken upon the wheel."

"Broken on the wheel?"

"Yes, for he had murdered his wife. As is the custom, he was forced to walk from the *Loch* to the *Rabenstein*, outside of the city, pinched by red-hot tongs along the way. Out of respect for my feelings, the Council limited application of the tongs to only two nips. Outside the Frauentor, he was allowed to receive the sacrament. At the Rabenstein, my brother and I had a meaningful discussion before I bound him to the wheel and administered the blows that would break his bones. At thirty-one strokes, he was finished."

"How terrible for him—and for you! Don't you ever want to escape your duties?"

"Of course. Dismembering the old woman today took all of my Warrior energy, but it had to be done. It was my duty."

"Has anyone tried to seek revenge on you?"

"Often. I dare not leave the city without a military escort, for many a Scharfrichter have been beset by mobs of peasants. Although I am skilled at my craft, I have failed to decapitate some poor soul with one blow, for example. Such mistakes incur the wrath of the crowd."

"Are there benefits to your job?"

"To be sure, a salary and fee for every punishment I administer. Torture is paid at half the rate of execution. I also receive gifts of money at the New Year and this rent-free house. Among the perks of this job is the opportunity to sell body parts, but I permit my Lion to conduct that trade. I prefer to pursue the trade of scribe for the illiterate. It takes my mind off the daily grind."

"How did you become a warrior?"

"The same way you will, Bob, by learning how and when to fight, by recognizing your duty, by refusing to compromise your values, and by accepting the consequences of your actions. Now you must go, before the Lion returns and discovers your disguise."

I had many more questions, but I sensed that the Scharfrichter had told me all he could. His Warrior energy, his values of duty, honor, and courage, were only one part of the puzzle I had to solve before I could return to my own time and place. He was still sitting on that wooden bench outside of his cottage near the Henkersteg when I crossed the Pegnitz and glanced over my shoulder before returning to Monk's quarters in the city wall.

CHAPTER FIVE

The Warrior Within

My return to Monk's hole in the wall was far more pleasant than that first, frenzied flight from the provisional posse. I was no longer obsessed with getting back to Merrill Barracks in time for bed check, reveille, or chow call. My "real" world, and life beyond the Army, would have to wait. A higher power than Sergeant Holmes had brought me to this time and place; I was sure of that. Monk, my mentor, would guide me through this world and return me to my own when I was ready.

Monk greeted me warmly and bade me to sit before the fire. Following a hearty meal of stew and brown farmer's bread, He poured wine and asked about my day. I told Him about my exploration of the city and that I had miraculously gained a working knowledge of the language. He nodded, knowingly. I then told about my experiences in the marketplace, the *Rathaus*, the *Loch*, and at the *Henkersteg*. I told Him about the old woman, her daughter and grandchild, the *Lion*, and the *Scharfrichter*. Monk was keenly interested in my conversation with the *Scharfrichter*, my questions, and His answers.

"Bob, why do your suppose you met the hangman, of all people?"

"He called Himself the Warrior."

"Why? Isn't a warrior a soldier who glories in battle?"

"I don't think so, Monk; He said that he didn't even like His job."

"Why would He do a job He doesn't like, Bob?"

"Well, He talked a lot about duty. Apparently, the Warrior does His duty, whether He likes it or not."

"Can you explain that a little more, Bob?"

"Okay, Let's say I'm on guard duty at Merrill Barracks. I spot a fellow

G.I. climbing the fence to sneak in after bed check. Hey, I don't really care if some drunk wants to avoid getting an Article 15 because he stayed '*on the Straße*' too late. He might turn out to be someone I know, or a friend of someone I know. I don't want people to hate me or even whip my ass 'cause I had to be all gung ho on guard duty. *I don't want to*, but I guess it would be my duty. I'm pretty sure that the Warrior would say so."

"I see. So, the Warrior is all about being a hard ass?"

"A hard ass? Yeah, maybe; at least, a Warrior has to act that way some-times. Still, I gotta think that there's more to it. Take me, for instance; I'm not some kind of gung-ho, Regular Army, son-of-a-bitch. I just want to get along with folks. To tell the truth, my real hero, growing up, was Jesus. I see myself as a gentle, kind, loving guy—not a hard ass."

"So you want to help people?"

"Yeah."

"Let's look at the example you described, Bob. A G.I. gets drunk downtown, and is afraid to get into trouble for missing bed check, so he climbs the fence, right?"

"Right."

"If you spot him and let him get away with it, what have you taught him?"

"Taught him?"

"Yes, Bob, we are all teachers. We teach one another how to behave by our own behavior and by our reactions to their behavior."

"Well, when you put it that way, I suppose I would teach the fence climber that military regulations don't really mean anything."

"Can you imagine any negative consequences of that lesson?"

"Oh sure, Monk, he would keep disregarding Army rules and orders from his superiors, and he would shirk his duty until he gets a dishon-orable discharge, maybe even some time in the stockade."

"So, in this case, being 'nice' to him by shirking your own duty would not be the same as doing what's best for him, right Bob?"

"You know, Monk, that's pretty much what the Warrior said."

"So, the Warrior talked about 'duty.' What else?"

"Honor."

"What is honor, Bob?"

"On the subject of honor, the hangman's actions spoke louder than his words. He showed compassion toward the old woman. He used a tourniquet to keep her from bleeding to death. He gave her strong wine to ease the pain. He carried out the magistrate's order to cut off the woman's left hand because of his duty to the rule of law. But he balanced his sense of duty with his sense of right and wrong. That was honorable. Maybe the magistrate was acting honorably too. The old woman might have been hanged or beheaded, as many thieves apparently are in this city, but he heeded her plea for mercy because her crime had been motivated by love for an innocent baby. Maybe honor means doing your best to do what's right—what you could explain to your mom, to your sergeant, to God, without shame."

"So if your mom would approve, it's probably honorable. I like that, Bob!"

"There's one more thing, Monk; when I asked the Warrior about his values, he listed duty, honor—and *courage*."

"When most people think of warriors—soldiers— courage comes to mind. The soldier must march into battle, not knowing whether he will return. To be afraid, but to face the danger anyway, takes real courage. What kind of courage does it take to lop off people's heads and hands?"

"The hangman did talk about certain physical dangers associated with his job. When you torture and execute people for a living, you make enemies, especially family and friends of the condemned. He can't go anywhere without guards. But he showed another kind of courage— a kind of mental, or emotional, courage."

"Really? Tell me about it, Bob."

"When I witnessed the old woman's punishment—hacking off her left hand—I felt only revulsion toward the hangman. He seemed no more emotionally involved than a butcher trimming a side of beef. He certainly did not seem courageous to me. In fact, I remember thinking, 'what a coward! That poor, helpless, old woman, held down by the brutish Lion!' That's how I felt at the time."

"But you said that he showed another kind of courage…"

"Yeah, but I didn't see it until afterward, when we were alone. The way he talked about the old woman, the tension he felt between duty and honor, and the empathy he felt for her, all convinced me that he confronted real fear that day."

"'Empathy?' That is an interesting word, Bob. What do you mean by it?"

"Well, he sort of put himself in her shoes, so to speak. He felt what she felt."

"Do you suppose that the hangman's empathy for the old woman was a unique case?"

"I don't think so, Monk; the Scharfrichter even told of the time he was obliged to execute his own brother. He made it clear that the question of guilt or innocence, and the punishment to be inflicted, are matters for the Council. He does not judge his victims…"

"So he is not motivated by revenge or righteous indignation…"

"Nope, only duty and honor. And yet, he knows exactly how much pain he will inflict from each kind of punishment: hanging, beheading, drowning, the wheel, or any type of torture. That's his job."

"Put that way, Bob, the Scharfrichter's ability to feel empathy for his victims, to feel their fear and pain, must be as great as the fear felt by a soldier going into combat."

"Maybe greater in some ways. It's natural to fear death, but when I joined the Army, my combat infantry training made death seem like a remote possibility. Deprived of sleep, I was in a perpetual daze; my critical thinking faculty was displaced by survival—the avoidance of punishment by officers and non-coms. I was conditioned, through repetition, to react to stimuli: commands from superiors, pop-up silhouettes on the range, the release of poison gas, and the low ceiling of live ammunition on the infiltration course. Basic training taught me to focus on immediate pain, such as the rocks tearing my elbows and knees, rather than the deadly fire overhead—or the possibility of death."

"But did you not consider the suffering of enemy combatants or innocent civilians you might encounter?"

"Actually, no, come to think of it. We were constantly reminded that, on the battlefield, our survival depended on killing the enemy, or anyone who could harm us. We were conditioned to think about 'targets,' not people."

"It sounds as though the Army did its best to insulate you from fear, as well as from empathy for the enemy."

"Yeah, I guess they do that so nice kids will not hesitate to kill if they find themselves in combat."

"Those punks who attacked a lone soldier outside your room needed no such brainwashing."

"You know, Monk, they must have been born innocent, cute little babies, but in the ghetto, they had to get tough fast—or die."

"They did not have the advantage of strong, male role models, Bob. The worst aspects of their Warrior went unchecked, resulting in a mere Shadow of the Warrior ideal. You will learn that for every essential quality of manhood, there is a flip side. Courage alone, without duty and honor, can produce evil."

"But for a man of conscience, like the Scharfrichter, the absence of conditioning by the Army or street gang permits him to feel empathy for the people sent to him. He understands and feels their fear and their pain..."

"Yet he does his duty for the greater good of society, even for the good of members of that society who may suffer the consequences of its canon."

"Exactly! And that's why I have come to feel that the Scharfrichter represents courage, along with his other professed values, duty and honor."

"Bob, do you now understand why I have arranged for you to meet this man?"

"The Scharfrichter called himself 'Warrior.' I hope that I can live up to the Warrior's values of duty, honor, and courage."

"This day has been a remarkable journey into your soul, Bob. You have learned your lesson well. You must keep the Warrior alive inside of you, leaving room for His comrades. Now, let us extinguish the candle and rest, for the morrow brings yet another task in your odyssey."

I slept for the second time in the Monk's grotto, that hole in the wall surrounding sixteenth-century Nuremberg, a time and place that would prepare me for the much more profound journey to come—life.

CHAPTER SIX

The Werkmeister

D awn roused me from dreams of carefree childhood—as a boy again, climbing my backyard cottonwood tree with tales of *Davy Crockett* tucked under my arm, reading for hours among the swaying branches. I explored my South Side neighborhood, hunting garter snakes along the railroad embankment and playing Robin Hood in the vacant lot we kids called "Sherwood Forest." On my bike, assembled from bits and pieces retrieved from neighbors' trash, I roamed far beyond my own block. I rode through Jackson Park, site of the *1893 World Columbian Exposition* and the fantastic *White City.* I cycled past the golden statue of *Columbia,* a reminder of the fair. I visited the Museum of Science and Industry, successor to the Palace of Fine Arts—the only permanent building of the exposition. In the 1950s, when admission was free, the museum had been a magnet for area kids, who could name each of the old-time airplanes hanging from the ceiling, knew every switch on the giant model railroad, and passed hours watching chicks hatch in the farm exhibit. We could tell the museum guards how to find any exhibit, in case they forgot. In my dream I rode once again to Rainbow Beach, the eastern edge of my South Side world. I hot-footed it across the burning sand, splashed in the cold, June water, gazed north along the shoreline to the city's downtown skyline, and tried to imagine what lay on the other side of that Great Lake. But now, along with dawn streaming through Monk's lone window, came a new day and a sense of anticipation. What adventure awaited me in that shining, sixteenth-century city on the hill?

As usual, Monk was up, preparing my breakfast and preparing me for my next challenge. Over strong tea, he talked about the changes taking place in Nürnberg.

"This city is in the vanguard of religious, artistic, and scientific changes sweeping Northern Europe," he said, "some of the greatest minds of our time are right here."

"The hangman was hardly a Renaissance Man," I reminded him.

"True Bob," said Monk, "but His values of duty, honor, and courage are timeless, as are the values of the men you have yet to meet."

"How many men have you arranged for me to meet, Monk?"

"Four total—the hangman and three more."

"Why four?"

"Bob, let's just say for now that each of these men has something to teach you before you are ready to return to your own time."

"Fair enough, Monk—I guess. I hope that one of them can teach me a good story to tell my commanding officer if I ever get back to Merrill Barracks."

"Don't be overly concerned with details such as that now, Bob. Your job, for the nonce, is to ask the right questions and to listen well."

"Got it, Monk. I can't wait for the next adventure."

Monk instructed me to return to the *Museumsbrücke,* where I had seen the Holy Ghost Hospital, and make my way to the construction site. "The hospital is being expanded to accommodate our growing population. Seek out the city *Werkmeister,* Hans Behaim. Be prepared to work." Monk provided me with a simple outfit to replace my monk's cassock—breeches and a tunic. My nascent familiarity with the language and customs contemporary to my setting would suffice for this peasant persona.

I retraced my route to the *Rathaus* but skirted the main market. Behind the Church of Our Lady, a little bridge took me to another island in the Pegnitz. I paused to gaze over the wide, park-like area to the east. Fragrant trees, wide lawns, and shrubs made it an oasis of green in this city of stone and timber. I even saw deer grazing in the meadow. I was entranced.

On my right, however, the scene was anything but idyllic. Dozens of workmen labored in the pale December sun. Carpenters and stonemasons pounded, lifted, and mortared from their perches on the scaffold. Their helpers carried materials to them on poles and in wheelbarrows. At the center of this commotion, a tall, distinguished man, in a sort of puffy beret and long, heavy cape, walked among the men, stopping now and again to inspect some detail of construction or provide advice. I presumed him to be the man Monk had called Hans Behaim, the superintendent of building construction for the city of Nürnberg. I waited until he returned to a rough-hewn table covered with drawings.

"*Guten Tag*, Herr Behaim," I said, bowing slightly.

"Ach, Bob, my new apprentice," he replied, smiling, "so you want to become a magician."

"I do?"

He laughed. "We in the Collective Unconscious have a flair for the dramatic. Not all magicians look like Merlin, with his pointed hat and magic wand."

"Are you a magician?"

"Hans Behaim, Magician, at your service. I am more prosaically known as master builder, architect, and Werkmeister, Superintendent of Building Construction for the Imperial city of Nürnberg. For the glory of its citizens and their God, I transform edifices such as the *Kornhaus*, the *Rathaus*, God's very own houses of worship, and this beautiful hospital, as if by magic."

I have to tell you, Alex, I was still confused. Why did the Monk send me to this man? Was I to learn about architecture? Magic? What did any of this have to do with me? How would it help me return to my own life—and to Gerdi? Was I permanently exiled to this new place and time?

"Excuse me, Mr. Behaim," I said, "I still don't understand."

"Of course not," he replied, "Few people do understand the arcana of my profession. That is precisely why I am a Magician."

"Well, what I mean, sir, is that I don't understand why I was sent to be your apprentice..."

"Wait here, while I check on my workers." The man made the rounds of the masons, carpenters, and other workers again. Then he returned to his log desk, rolled up some drawings, and motioned for me to follow him. We walked around to the Museumsbrücke, where Mr. Behaim studied the facade of the Holy Ghost Hospital. Satisfied with his progress, he led me on a tour of his architectural accomplishments in the city. He seemed especially proud of renovation projects

The Holy Ghost Hospital

that added beauty and utility to existing structures. "Always build upon what exists, Bob," he remarked, when I asked him why he incorporated part of a former city wall into the Kornhaus. Was he referring only to architecture? I wondered. I made a note to ask him about that if the opportunity arose.

Eventually, we arrived at his home in the *St. Sebald* quarter. The street level appeared to be a workshop and studio. I was drawn to the detailed models of Mr. Behaim's architectural projects. One model in particular was breathtaking—the entire city of Nürnberg, showing the wall, the castle, the streets, and buildings. Thinking of my own half-finished plastic model cars at home, I marveled at the patience and unflagging commitment required for such a project. I was beginning to sense that this man might, indeed, have something to teach me.

"You seem to be intrigued by these prototypes, Bob."

"Yes sir. I am impressed by the effort you put into the models of your projects."

"Actually, they are not all my projects. In some cases, I had to sketch and construct the surrounding structures to see how mine would fit in. There is beauty in harmony."

Thinking of the hodgepodge of buildings on 79th Street, I realized that my world could learn some things from the study of history. "How did you become the Werkmeister of Nürnberg?" I asked.

"That is an excellent question, young man," said Mr. Behaim, "You have the makings of an excellent apprentice. Asking the right questions is essential. I am prepared to entertain all of your questions, but first, let us sup before the fire."

In contrast to Monk's simple fare, or Army mess hall chow, the supper served by Mr. Behaim's cook was plentiful and delicious. We had spicy pork sausage, served with sauerkraut and sweet cakes filled with crabmeat, washed down with several mugs of delicious beer. *(Sorry, Mom, but this was the best meal I had ever eaten.)*

Afterward, Mr. Behaim lit a pipe and fixed me with an imposing, but kindly expression. He seemed to be more curious about me than I was about him. "You asked me how I became Werkmeister, Bob. Before I tell you my story, tell me your story."

Taken off guard, I replied that I came from a working family in a city called Chicago, in America, in the twentieth century.

"America!" He knew of America from stories being told by Spanish explorers. "How is it that your appearance resembles that of my contemporaries, Bob? We hear tales of a brown race of men who inhabit America."

I explained that I am descended from European immigrants to America.

"And you came here from the future you say?"

"More than five hundred years in the future, Herr Behaim."

"I was told to expect you, Bob, but forgive me; I must know more! How did it happen? How do you come to understand our language? How do people live in your time? What do they do with themselves? What are their buildings like? How do they make war? How do they travel? How do they…"

And so our dialogue began. The Magician's thirst for knowledge provoked my own curiosity. His questions about science and technology in the twentieth century caused me to reflect upon matters I had always taken for granted: How did "flying machines," as he called them, work? How are the images and voices of people broadcast around the world? How could the energy in a liquid taken from the ground transport people faster than a real horse? What are these invisible things called germs that make people ill? I was unable to explain these mysteries to his satisfaction. "Only certain people, scientists, engineers and physicians, for example, understand how these things work," I said.

"Ah, the magicians," said Herr Behaim.

"Oh, now I get it," I said, "when you refer to yourself as 'Magician,' it's because you know about architecture and building, things the average person doesn't know."

"Precisely, Bob! Moreover, the Magician lives inside of you, waiting to be discovered."

"But I have never even considered architecture."

"Architecture is *my* magic, Bob, but the Magician manifests Himself in the physician's dosing, the artisan's craft, the scholar's philosophy. Look around you, Bob; the city of Nürnberg is flowering with Magician energy: science, craft, enterprise, and art! The Magician is that part of your soul that compels you to seek truth, to ask questions, to master a small part of the universe."

"Like architecture?"

"Yes, Bob, or perhaps, in your day, the magic of traveling pictures and words."

I considered Herr Behaim's words and thought about the signals I sent and received as an Army radio teletype operator. Had I ever gone beyond the "how-to" of my military training in signal school to learn how those signals got from my keyboard, telegraph key, or microphone to their destination? No. Why not? Surely, among the dusty shelves in the post library, there must be books that explained the physics of wave propagation, that described oscillators, amplifiers, and other electronics circuits used in my work. Could the Magician that Herr Behaim spoke about help me to learn such things? Would such knowledge help me to fulfill my role as a man, a husband, father, and provider, in my own time? I was beginning to understand Monk's purpose in sending me to Herr Behaim.

"How did you become a magician?" I asked.

"Earlier, you asked how I became the Werkmeister of Nürnberg. That was a good question. In order to answer it, however, I must address your second question first, for the honor and privilege bestowed upon the Magician is a consequence of His magic. I shall reveal to you the secrets of that magic if you are ready to learn."

"I am ready, sir," I replied.

"The Magician is inquisitive; the Magician is committed to a life of study; and the Magician is courageous."

"I could tell that you are curious because of your questions about my life in twentieth century America," I said.

"Of course! What an extraordinary opportunity to learn! Can you imagine anyone not brimming with curiosity about such things?"

I thought of the Scharfrichter, and his values: duty, honor, and courage—values I would do my best to internalize. Yet, curiosity had been conspicuously absent. He had not questioned the accuracy or morality of sentences he had been ordered to carry out. Apparently, Warrior energy was necessary, but not sufficient to accomplish my mission in this very foreign territory. "How can I develop the inquisitive approach to life that you have, Herr Behaim?"

"Ah, but you need only to get in touch with that child that you once were, that child who peppered his mother and father with questions about his world."

Alex, as I'm telling you this story, I am reminded of when you were a toddler, exploring your world, just learning to talk. Your favorite words were, "What's that?" which you pronounced, "wazat?" I would tell you the name, and you would then turn to something new: "Wazat?" You were a sponge, soaking up knowledge of your environment: "Wazat?" "Wazat?" "Wazat?"

"I think I understand, Herr Behaim, I said, "Curiosity comes naturally to a child. But kids stop asking all those annoying questions as they get older."

"Yes. Parents or teachers may feel dumb if they cannot answer a question. They become impatient if the question interrupts them in the middle of a task. They may dismiss the question, teaching the child not to ask questions. As children, we learn those behaviors that are rewarded, such as keeping quiet and doing what the adult wants."

"But your parents did not discourage your curiosity?"

"They considered it natural. They encouraged me to question everything. They thought of possible answers to my questions and asked what I thought about those answers. We often tested our ideas. My father and I once spent days playing with rocks in the stream behind our little home, making bridges. The Holy Ghost Hospital spans the Pegnitz much as one of our designs spanned that little stream."

I thought of the graceful arches of the Holy Ghost Hospital and the river flowing under them. "Millions of people still admire your design in the twentieth century, Herr Behaim."

Herr Behaim smiled. "It all started with a question—and play."

"It's interesting that you mention play, Herr Behaim; we associate play with children."

"As we do curiosity."

"Yes."

"Bob, that is because the Magician is, at heart, a child. He looks at the world as a puzzle, a game. He is amazed by the sight of a rainbow, the movement of stars, the shape of a leaf, a snake shedding its skin. He strives to understand these things and delights in discovery."

"But Herr Behaim, how does a curious child discover the answers to such questions?"

"The Magician is impelled by His curiosity; He seeks truth with the zeal of a pirate seeking gold. The world is His ship, His mentor is the captain; a scholar's treatise is His treasure map."

"The way you describe it—a ship, a captain, a map—it sounds like a journey."

"It is, Bob, a lifelong quest for answers. Like Odysseus, the Magician travels far beyond His comfort zone, into unknown territory, encountering bizarre challenges and overcoming them with sagacity and courage."

"You spoke of a mentor, Herr Behaim; would that be something like a teacher?"

"Yes, Bob. Actually, the Magician may have many mentors in His lifetime. His parents, like my own sweet mother and father, are the first. I have told you how they encouraged my questions and stimulated my curiosity about the world."

"Did you go to school in Nürnberg?"

"Yes, I attended the Trivial School of *St. Lorenz*, so-called because we studied *The Trivium*. It was a good school. We learned Latin, of course, but most importantly, we learned reading, writing, and math."

"Math must be important to you as a builder."

"Of course, Bob; it is a tool for constructing buildings, ships, or any kind of machinery on paper. If I can construct a mathematical model of my idea that withstands rigorous analysis, I then have the courage to propose that project to the Council, to order the material required, and to direct construction of it.

"Mr. Behaim," I said, "I have always considered mathematics to be an analytical tool. Now you speak of courage—an emotion."

"Courage is, indeed, required by the Magician—a courage born of confidence. The precision of mathematics undergirds that confidence. As my apprentice, you will learn firsthand about courage. But there is more to mathematics, Bob; it is a language—a very precise, universal language—to communicate with other Magicians, past, present, and future."

"Magicians have their own language?"

"Magicians do have a special language they use within their own realms. A fellow architect understands me when I speak of merlons or brattices, for example, but those words mean nothing to a Magician who is heir to Aesculapius. Likewise, physicians speak to one another of lavage or of nosocomial, terms foreign to my ears, even as I build the

Holy Ghost Hospital in Nürnberg. In addition to the argot of their specialized realm, all Magicians share the universal languages of scholars: mathematics, Latin, and Greek."

"Okay, but how do we ordinary folks communicate with Magicians?"

"Splendid question, Bob! The glorious magic worked by those of us who devote our lives to it must not remain secret. We Magicians are also human beings, with the aspirations, emotions, and frailties of all flesh and blood. We learned the language of our mothers before we learned the language of our magic. Just as we build bridges to connect the people on opposite sides of a river, so must we build bridges between people, with their needs and desires, and our magical solutions."

"That word—'bridge'—is a good example of using something familiar to make an abstract concept concrete," I said. "I think it's called a metaphor."

"Language is an important part of that magic that connects all human beings, Bob—communication. We all communicate with words, with gestures and actions, with mathematical symbols, with drawings, and with the artifacts we construct. In a real sense, everyone who has ever lived, or who will ever live, is part of the same enterprise—civilization. I have made a reputation for building on the works of others. The Kornhaus incorporates part of a former city wall; indeed, I have contributed to the present wall that protects our city. The project we are currently undertaking is an expansion of the Holy Ghost Hospital, not a new building at all. But the fact is, all human accomplishment is built on a foundation laid by others. That is how communication binds us together over time and distance."

"And that's what you meant when you said that the scholar's treatise is the Magician's treasure map?"

"Right, Bob, and the world His ship. His mentor is the captain of that ship."

"So, your mentors have been your parents, your teachers, and predecessors…"

"Yes, Bob, and my colleagues and patrons with whom I collaborate even today."

"It sounds as though you are saying that mentors can be anywhere."

"Anyone who answers my questions, who teaches me, is my mentor."

You have helped me to understand that the Magician is inquisitive, and he is committed to lifelong learning, but I still don't understand the part about courage. I thought that was part of the Warrior."

Our conversation had gone on for hours. Herr Behaim suggested that we get some sleep. "Tomorrow, you will be my apprentice, Bob, and you may have the opportunity to answer your own question."

Herr Behaim showed me to my sleeping quarters, a large, comfortable room on the third floor. A fire burned in the hearth. My window overlooked a dark city street, silent at that post-curfew hour. I lay on the featherbed, and soon *Hypnos*, the god of sleep, carried me away on that fluffy, white, cloud.

The sounds of a rising city stirred me from a magical dream. In it, my first bicycle, rescued from a neighbor's trash, lay in pieces before me like a jigsaw puzzle: the triangular frame, the rusty wheels, the grimy chain, the handlebars (wide, like the long horns of a steer), and the worn seat, with its two coiled springs. I painted the frame a royal blue, applying pin stripe decals to the fenders and chain guard. I polished the handlebars and covered the worn seat with a white seat cover. I used metal polish and fine steel wool on the rims and every spoke until they looked almost new. I soaked the chain in fuel oil to remove dirt from its bearings. I did the same with the hub from the front wheel, using a short-bristled brush. All that was tedious, but easy. The final challenge, the one I dreaded, was to disassemble the rear axel and New Departure brake. The brake mechanism consisted of numerous small parts: washers, bearings, clutch, and sprocket. If even one of these parts was left out or put back incorrectly, the result would be disaster.

I called upon my childhood mentor, my hero—my big brother—for help. He patiently showed me how to spread a large, clean cloth on the ground, so none of the tiny parts would get lost. He told me to use paper and pencil to diagram the assembly. He said to count the number of threads on the axle as I came to each part, to make lots of notes, to feel how the parts on the complicated mechanism move before removing them, and to lay all the parts out on the cloth in order. As my dream unfolded, I saw myself doing as my brother instructed—cleaning and lubricating the parts, reassembling the brake, and putting the whole bicycle together again. I felt the tires getting hard as I pumped them up and the proper amount of play in the chain as I adjusted the rear wheel. I adjusted the seat and handlebars. Finally, I mounted my bicycle, resurrected from oblivion and rebuilt as good as new—better, in fact, with its custom paint job and pin stripes. I rode around the block, passing other kids on store-bought three-speed "racers." That bike was a part of me, built from the magic of imagination, determination, careful study, and a guiding mentor. As I skidded to a stop in the alley where my brother was waiting, I said, "Thank you, Mentor." As sometimes happens in dreams, my brother turned into the figure of *Morpheus*, the god of dreams.

"You're welcome," came the voice of Herr Behaim, "but your apprenticeship with me is not over yet. Today you work." I blinked open my eyes to sunlight streaming in through the east window of my room in Hans Behaim's house.

Following a breakfast of bread, something like oatmeal, cheese, and beer(!), Mr. Behaim suggested that I put on a pair of breeches and a waistcoat, and we ventured out onto the street. As we walked, he pointed with pride to the cobblestone streets. Nary a stone was out of place. As city architect, Herr Behaim was responsible for the maintenance of streets, along with his other duties. He made daily inspections, ordering repairs to be carried out by paving masters, their journeymen, apprentices, and laborers.

"Even with so many people actually working on the streets, they look remarkably consistent," I said, thinking of streets in the city of my childhood—concrete, asphalt, brick, and sometimes all three on the same street.

"It is my responsibility to specify the size and quality of paving stones," Herr Behaim said, "and the number of blows each must receive from the pounder."

Presently, we arrived at the Museumsbrücke, where we could observe workers already at work on the Holy Ghost Hospital renovation. Herr Behaim spread his drawings out on a table and instructed me to study them while he made his rounds.

Remembering my dream, in which I had conquered the New Departure braking mechanism on my first bicycle, I compared the architect's drawings to the building under construction before me. I considered the river Pegnitz, flowing under graceful arches of the hospital's foundation. I walked to the edge of the Pegnitz. I picked up a long, stout stick and waded into the river to feel its current. I used the stick to measure its depth at various points. I observed the high water marks on the abutments of the Museumsbrücke. I used my stick to dig into the building site; I wanted to know more about the kind of soil, its depth and compactness. I walked under the scaffold surrounding the building, picking up stones and other materials, measuring the thickness of walls with my stick, and observing construction techniques and the techniques used by the carpenters and masons.

Returning to Herr Behaim's desk, I recorded my observations on the reverse of one of Herr Behaim's drawings. I sat quite still on a large stone bench, meditating. Drawing on the process that had enabled me to assimilate the sixteenth century German language from the depths of the Collective Unconscious, I summoned from the past my high school physics. It penetrated my consciousness slowly, like a photograph developing in its chemical bath. Herr Behaim returned.

"Well, what have you learned, Bob?"

"I have studied your design, Herr Behaim," I stammered, "and it is a beautiful concept..."

"I think that there is something on your mind, young man," said the Great One.

I replied, "It is nothing, sir." How could I tell this man, Herr Hans Behaim, chief builder for the City of Nürnberg, that he had made a fatal miscalculation? What made me think that I, a visitor to this historical period, a kid with no training in architecture, could possibly have anything to contribute to this project?

"Nothing?" said Herr Behaim, "Why is your face flushed" Why do your hands tremble? Why does your tongue stammer if it is nothing?"

"I am sorry, sir, but my disoriented, foolish mind is confused. I do not understand one part of your great plan for this structure."

"And what part might that be?"

"Well, here, sir," I said, pointing to a detail on one of the drawings, "I believe that the river, flowing at its crest, will undermine the arch brick unless the embedded columns are extended and buttressed."

Herr Behaim's countenance changed; I couldn't tell whether he was going to laugh or strike me. After an excruciating silence, he said, "Show me."

I sketched my calculations of the river's volume and force, using diagrams and equations to support my conclusion.

Herr Behaim watched and listened carefully. He then handed me a marker and said, "Make your change on the drawing, and construction will proceed accordingly."

Now I was really terrified! Was Herr Behaim giving me the responsibility for making a structural change to the Holy Ghost Hospital, a building that would become known to millions of people in the coming centuries? What would my changes mean to the cost and timetable of construction? What if I was wrong? What if the building collapsed? He waited patiently. I drew lines over his, raising and fortifying the columns on which the entire building would rest.

Herr Behaim's face broke into a wide smile. "Congratulations, Bob, you just learned the meaning of courage, an essential trait of the Magician." He motioned to the stone bench and sat down beside me. Speaking softly, he said, "The Magician is inquisitive, curious. He notices and thinks about things that others take for granted. He asks, 'why?' Unlike a *dilettante*, who has only a superficial interest in the arts and sciences, the Magician makes a lifelong commitment to study, to finding answers to questions. But if a man does nothing more, he is merely an egghead. The Magician goes beyond contemplation; He engages his fellow man, His world, and all the creatures in it. He asks the right questions; He seeks the right answers; and He applies His magic to the glory of God on earth. That takes courage. You struggled with yourself to employ your own magic—your hard-won knowledge of physics, your talent for observation and analysis—to this project. You conquered your fear of failure, your aversion to conflict, when you challenged me, the great city builder. Now I shall share with you a secret aspect of the Magician that calls for another kind of courage."

My initial relief that Herr Behaim had not freaked out about the changes I suggested gave way to puzzlement. I understood what he meant about overcoming the fear of failure, for I had just experienced that, but what was this about another aspect of Magician energy? "You're not mad about my ideas for the building?" I asked.

"No, Bob, and I shall tell you why. The design you modified was actually submitted by a very clever rival of mine, the *Trickster*. When His proposal to the Council was rejected in favor of mine, he disguised Himself as an apprentice mason and reported to this job site. During a period of great activity following the erection of the scaffolding, he moved a plank being used by workmen to wheel material to the river's edge. The plank gave way, and a man fell into the Pegnitz. Using that as a diversion, my rival substituted his drawing for mine. According to His scheme, I would not notice the switch; construction would proceed, and no one would notice, until it was too late, that His design, rather than mine, had prevailed."

"And He would take over your job as city as Werkmeister for the City of Nürnberg, right?"

"Yes, that was His plan. Fortunately, I remain open to criticism—self-criticism as well as criticism from others. The Magician is not arrogant. There is always opportunity for improvement. Thus it was, as I was reviewing my plans for the Holy Ghost Hospital, that I noticed the supplanted drawing. That was shortly after the 'accidental' dousing of the workman in the Pegnitz. I inferred the connection and exposed the saboteur. The Council consigned my clever, but deceitful rival to the *Scharfrichter* to be whipped out of town."

I shuddered, remembering the hangman's conscientious but unquestioning obedience to authority. "It's a good thing you caught His trick, Herr Behaim, otherwise the hospital might have collapsed when the Pegnitz reached flood stage."

"Yes, Bob, and for your sake, I am pleased that you demonstrated the courage of your convictions. Remember, your Magician will guide you to the right questions, the right answers, and the courage to act upon that knowledge in the right way."

"You're saying that I should use my brain for good, not for greed."

"Never dishonor the Magician, Bob."

I thanked Herr Behaim and took my leave. Monk would be keen to hear of my encounter with the Magician. When I reached the path leading from the island known as *Insel Schütt* to the vicinity of the marketplace, a man dressed in the manner of carpenters I had seen working on the hospital renovation approached. "Good day, young man," he said. "You seem to be familiar with the Holy Ghost Hospital construction project. Would you like to earn a tidy sum for a few minutes' work?"

As a matter of fact, the lack of money had been an issue for me since my appearance in this alien world. My only meals had been provided by Monk and Herr Behaim. I was curious. "Perhaps, kind stranger," I replied, "What is required of me?"

"Simply this," answered the man, "take this message to my foreman, the lead carpenter at the hospital work site."

"What is it," I asked.

"That is none of your business, young man. Besides, you would not understand the symbols and special terms we carpenters use. I shall pay you *28 d*—a day's wage for a journeyman carpenter."

That sounded very generous—too generous. I said, "Please, sir, allow a simple young man to behold the designs of a great builder! Though your mysterious words and symbols may be far beyond my comprehension, the honor of beholding their sacred beauty will be a memory I shall share with my children and grandchildren."

The man, taken in by my flattery, relented. "Feast your peasant eyes on the work of a genius, and tell your scions that you once met the greatest architect in Nürnberg!" With that, he handed me a small scroll.

At once, I recognized its significance. It contained instructions that would sap the foundations of the Holy Ghost Hospital! I feigned admiration for the document and gazed at its author. His gleaming black eyes and tiny ears gave me a chill. Fresh welts on his hands and face made me suspect that he was Herr Behaim's rival, who had been whipped out of town. Disguised as a carpenter, he was now bent on revenge. The foreman of carpenters must have been in league with him. I bowed and said that I would deliver the document to the proper person.

That evening, having taken my leave of the Werkmeister, I recounted to Monk my conveyance of the treacherous plan to Herr Behaim, the subsequent arrest of the conspirators, and their confinement to the Loch, awaiting trial and punishment.

CHAPTER SEVEN

The Magician Within

"**A**re you beginning to understand my purpose in bringing you to this time and place, Bob?"

"A little," I said, "at least, I got the impression that there's a lot of creative energy in Nürnberg these days. Exploring the city, I saw it everywhere—in the churches, of course, and in other public buildings, but also in the crafts and instruments for sale in the marketplace."

"Each of those artisans and inventors is, in his own way, a magician, Bob."

"Yeah, I see that now, but I'm not sure what it has to do with me."

Monk smiled and handed me a mug of strong tea. "Let's sit before the fire and see what the dancing flames can show us." We sat on his rough, wooden bench, close to the fireplace, sipping tea. "Now, just relax, Bob, and let your mind see what it will."

Feeling warm and safe, my hunger satisfied by Monk's simple fare, I drifted into a kind of trance. It was as though I was back home, a boy again, staring into a campfire in the vacant lot next door. Billy was there, and Jimmy. We were talking, as boys do, about what we would be when we grew up.

"I'm going to be a cop," said Billy, "like my uncle. He gets to carry a gun."

"Yeah?" Said Jimmy, "Did he ever shoot anyone?"

"Oh yeah, lots of times," said Billy, "at least, I think so. He doesn't like to talk about stuff like that."

Jimmy looked skeptical. "Aw, I bet he never did. He probably just snags speeders and writes tickets if they don't have a five dollar bill clipped to their license."

Billy sprang to his feet: "You want to fight about it?"

"Jimmy didn't mean it," I had said, "He's just kidding. Right, Jimmy?"

"Yeah, yeah," said Jimmy, "I was just kidding. I wish my old man was like your uncle. All he does is go around to taverns, selling beer."

Billy sat down again, apparently mollified by Jimmy's disparaging description of his own father's business. We all knew that Jimmy's dad was almost rich; he had a new Chevy and a cottage in Wisconsin. Billy didn't have a dad. "What about you, Bob? Are you going to get a job in the mills?"

My dad worked in the steel mills. He took the South Chicago Avenue bus to work every morning when the mills were not on strike. When they were on strike, he drank beer and fought with my mom. It seemed to me that they were always on strike. "Maybe," I said. "I don't really know."

"Don't you ever think about stuff like that?" asked Jimmy, "...like being a fireman, or a cowboy, or...."

"Naw—well, sometimes I think about being a minister." I attended Sunday school, church, and B.Y.F. —Baptist Youth Fellowship—as a kid. I read my Bible every day. My heroes were Jesus and my big brother. The minister was the only adult male I ever talked to.

Billy put another "log" on the fire—actually a scrap of 2x4 from the neighbor's trashcan. "A minister? Hell, you can't even talk!" Billy was sort of the Huckleberry Finn of my crowd. He liked to get my goat by saying things like "hell."

That hurt, because it was true. My speech defect isolated me from most kids. I didn't know how I could be a minister and preach every Sunday. I didn't feel like fighting, so I left my only friends at the campfire and walked away, sobbing a little.

"Let him go," said Jimmy, "he's just a crybaby."

Recalling that long-ago scene, I remembered thinking, "I'll show them! I'll show everyone. I'll read; I'll study hard in school. I'll get so smart that people will beg me to work for them, even if I can't talk." By the time I got home, I felt better. I climbed the cottonwood tree behind my house with my library book, a biography of George Washington Carver. There, far above the childish squabbles of my peers, I learned how one man was able to free himself from hardship and prejudice through his curiosity about the peanut, through diligent study, and by using his knowledge for the good of mankind.

Mentor gently broke into my reverie. "You could have become a minister, you know."

"Yeah, the church actually offered me a scholarship to Moody Bible Institute, but I didn't take it. How could I, when I couldn't even talk?"

"The Marine Corps told you that your wouldn't be able to pick up a walkie-talkie and call for help if your squad was wiped out, but now you are a radio operator in the Army."

"Yeah, kind of funny, isn't it?"

"The point is, Bob, you will be surprised what life has in store for you."

"You mean you know?"

"Yes, Bob, but I am not saying. Your life is your own, to discover for yourself."

"So, if you don't mind, Mentor, can you tell me what I'm supposed to accomplish here, before I can get back to the real world?"

"Do you remember the Boy Scout motto, Bob?"

"Sure, 'Be Prepared!' My regimental motto is the same, only in French: 'Toujours Pret.'"

"Hmm…there is a subtle difference, Bob. 'Toujours Pret' means, 'always ready.' That's a statement. The Scout motto, 'Be Prepared!' is an exhortation. You are not quite ready to fulfill your mission as a fully developed man in the twentieth century."

"So you are going to help me to be prepared. You know, I was just thinking about that as we were looking into the fire, maybe because you sent me to work with Hans Behaim, the *Werkmeister*, a sort of magician…"

"Yes, Herr Behaim represents the Magician energy that you will need to shape the wonders of your own time, just as Hephaistos shaped wondrous implements for the gods in his fiery forge. Let us see what the flames have to say about that…"

Once more, we gazed silently at the hearth, where logs, which had once been living tree branches, shifted and collapsed in the fire, changing shape, and combining with flame and shadow to form images. In the flying sparks I saw electrical energy lighting the world; in a plume of smoke, terrible destruction. Suddenly, a log tilted to the vertical, its bottom end catching fire like a rocket on the launching pad. Shadows dancing about the fire conjured up images: a '56 Ford, cars of all shapes and sizes. I listened to the crackling sticks. There seemed to be a pattern to the sound; was it the Morse Code I had learned in signal school? No, there were no dashes, only dots. But it was some kind of code. Listening carefully, I discerned a sequence based on time—measures of time. If each measure were divided into four beats, the beat would have a dot or no dot. I tapped my foot in time and counted: dot-tap-tap-tap/dot-tap-tap-dot/tap-dot-dot-tap/tap-dot-dot-tap. That pattern repeated it-self over and over. What did it mean? What did any of this mean? Was I seeing my future, the future of civilization?

"Yes," said Mentor, reading my thoughts again. It was spooky how He could do that. "Yes, you are seeing your own future and the future of civilization. Your own century will be a time of great advances in sci-ence and technology, advances the best minds of our Renaissance can only dream of. They dream of traveling between great cities in thunder-ing caravans of iron wagons on iron roads. They dream of darting about the land in smaller wagons, pulled by no beast. They dream of flying like birds, even to the moon. They dream of invisible fire that can turn night into day. They dream of sending their voices, and even images, around the world. They dream of combining their great minds into a master brain, a source of infinite knowledge, to be used for the benefit of mankind..."

"Or its destruction," I added, thinking of the nuclear weapons trained by the U.S. and the U.S.S.R. on each other.

"Or its destruction," Monk conceded, "but my point, Bob, is that these things, which Magicians of this century only dream of, will be-come a reality in your own time. As a twentieth-century man, you must be a Magician; you have no choice."

"So that's what you wanted me to see in the fire—the magic of my world?"

"Yes; the magical energy that was confined to the shaman in primi-tive societies and is found in the artists, explorers, inventors, and build-ers today—men like Hans Behaim—will be an essential survival skill for you. That is why you met the Werkmeister."

"So it was not to learn the secrets of his trade?"

"No, Bob, it was to learn the secrets of his magic."

"Curiosity, commitment, and courage—those are the things Herr Behaim spoke of."

"Those are magical qualities that transcend time, Bob. Let us take one last look into the flames, to see how."

Once again, Mentor and I turned toward the fire. Once again, its warmth and the hypnotic flickering of its flames lulled me to a state of tranquil awareness. The popping and crackling of burning sticks produced once more that strange code: dot-tap-tap-tap/dot-tap-tap-dot/tap-dot-dot-tap/tap-dot-dot-tap. I saw myself, as if I were watching a home movie, deciphering the code on a blackboard: dot-tap-tap-tap: one-zero-zero-zero. Dot-tap-tap-dot: one-zero-zero-one. Tap-dot-dot-tap: Zero-one-one-zero. Tap-dot-dot-tap: Zero-one-one-zero. My mind raced; only two numbers, one and zero—could that be it? Wait a minute! Could this code be based on that numbering system computers use? What's it called, "octal?" There was something in one of those magazines at the base library about it… Trying to remember, I played with the coded pops being emitted over and over by the fire. I came up with 1,966, a strange number indeed, until I removed the comma: 1966—the year I would be discharged by the Army. That would be the beginning of my adult life, I suppose, if the Army were really an extension of childhood, like college. What else might happen in 1966?

Continuing to stare into the fire as if it were a crystal ball, I saw the pile of wood burn and collapse, causing two branches to approach each other and appear to fuse. The resulting flame produced two smaller flames. I saw my own image again, donning Merlin's hat and scooping the flames into my arms, holding it close to my chest. I saw sparks fly from my fingers, circling my head. A great light shone round about. The crackling and popping began again. Dots and taps, ones and zeros, filled the space above my head with octal code, raining down upon me. Their sharp edges struck my skull, causing me pain and making me dizzy. I grasped groups of ones and zeros as if they were pieces of a jigsaw puzzle, arranging them into a pattern that formed a great mural along the wall of an endless corridor. From the darkened end of the corridor came a shadowy figure, a terrible, frightening monster, rearranging the elements of my mural. I pursued the monster into the darkness, repairing His trickery. As the Shadow receded, light poured into the darkest corners of the corridor. Many people, young and old, men and women, walked the corridor, admiring the mural, which was brilliant.

These images and sounds, emanating from the fire, were as vivid as if they had appeared on a high definition television, Alex.

CHAPTER EIGHT

How I Met My King

O n Monday of the following week, I exited Monk's dim lair within the city wall with instructions to witness the arrival of Emperor Charles V for the 1522 *Diet,* or assembly of governors, of
the Holy Roman Empire. I shielded my eyes from the brilliant sunlight.
It was a perfect day for the pageantry of the emperor's procession—
quite mild for January. The brown, hooded, ankle-length, wool cassock
I wore over my G.I. fatigues—a gift from the monk, to disguise my alien
identity—was plenty warm. From the covered, wooden catwalk outside
Monk's door, I looked down upon narrow, cobblestone streets, zigzag-
ging toward the main thoroughfare that would become *Königstraße* in
my own time. Those streets were filled with excited Nürnbergers, proud
that their city was to host the royal Diet.

For weeks, bishops, princes, margraves, and other important per-
sonages had been arriving in Nürnberg for the Diet. The *Golden Bull* of
1356 decreed that the first Diet of each newly crowned emperor must
be held at Nürnberg, foremost among the imperial free cities of the
Holy Roman Empire.

The *Bürgermeister* and city council made sure that their city was
even more splendid than usual for this occasion. The gates of the great
city wall were opened to permit peasants of the surrounding countryside to join with patricians, artisans, and other citizens of Nürnberg in
welcoming Charles V. *Königstraße* (as I would know it in the 1960s), the
route taken by Charles and other visiting dignitaries, was given special attention. Residents were ordered to scrub the streets in front of
their buildings. Balconies were to be festooned with red and white, the
city colors. The practice of driving pigs through the street to bathe in

the Pegnitz River was suspended. Jews were forced from the central marketplace and confined to their homes on *Judenstraße*. Their modest stalls in the market were displaced by an elaborate display of relics normally stored in the sanctuary of *St. Sebaldus*: preserved fingers of unnamed saints, splinters reputed to be from the cross of Jesus, and stones from the temple of Jerusalem.

I followed the rough-hewn timbered catwalk inside the sandstone city wall to a set of stairs leading to an alley below. Soon I was caught up in the throng of people making their way to *Königstraße*. The sounds of vendors selling beer, wine, and sausages from their carts filled the air.

The smell of their wares, blended with that of the people, was raw—like the time you and I tried to eat hot dogs while we inspected elephants at the circus. Remember, Alex?

Spectators stood four deep on either side of *Königstraße* at the *Marktplatz*, so I joined the people seeking a better spot farther up the parade route. From the main marketplace on the north bank of the Pegnitz, this street narrowed and became increasingly steep as it climbed to the highest point in Nürnberg, the castle hill.

The rocky outcrops of the castle hill offered a splendid view of the parade route. One could easily follow the emperor's open carriage as it slowly approached the imperial castle. I selected a good spot, but the crush of *Bürgers* was oppressive; my modern senses were not yet accustomed to sixteenth-century standards of hygiene. To get away from the overpowering body odor, I climbed a spindly oak tree of the type that one sometimes sees growing miraculously among scraggly boulders. Gathering the hem of my cassock, I perched on a low-hanging branch, now bare of foliage, and settled in to await the royal procession.

People were everywhere—lining the parade route, overlooking the street from windows and balconies, standing on the parapets of the city's formidable wall, and peering through the battlements of the castle itself. Some sang loudly, toasting one another with draughts of wine and beer. Others, caught up in the excitement of that momentous day, milled about like New Year's Eve celebrants in Times Square.

Before long, sounds of cheering in the distance announced the royal procession. The cheering grew louder, and the crowd in the street parted for a troop of horsemen—the emperor's guard! The guards pushed people aside with their horses and long poles. Most of the people on the castle hill below me surged forward, impatient for their first glimpse of Charles V. ("How silly," I thought, "we will have a perfect view of the procession as it enters the castle grounds from these boulders up here on the hill.") One fellow, however, moved away from the street to a position behind the bolder under my tree limb. He did not notice me, for his attention was focused on the procession. Curious, I watched him. He appeared ordinary enough—neither an artisan nor a patrician—possibly a peasant from the countryside, I speculated, noting his broad shoulders, simple, black coat, and leather knapsack. His behavior, however, was very different from that of the other spectators. He did not smile. He did not cheer, yet his intense gaze scanned the crowd, the emperor's guards, and the parade route. "What a strange bird," I thought. (But then again, I must have looked strange myself, perched in that tree.)

At last, the main procession came into view! More guards, pike men on foot, preceded the carriage of Charles V, drawn by eight powerful, bay horses. I could see the emperor perfectly as his carriage approached the castle. I was so excited! The man below me stirred. He's excited too, I thought. As the pike men marched by and the emperor's open carriage passed directly in front of my position, I leaned forward on the branch for a better look. Just then, the man below me shouted something—something angry—and removed a device that looked like a crossbow from his knapsack. Startled, I lost my balance. I fell from my branch, landing on the man just as he released an arrow.

The emperor's carriage stopped, and his pike men rushed toward us. The mounted guards executed a precise maneuver to keep the crowd at bay. The emperor's guards looked quite different from the ragged, citizen posse that had accosted me when I first emerged from that tunnel leading to the twentieth century in my G.I fatigues. These men were disciplined, fearless professionals. I scrambled to my feet and put my hands in the air.

The officer in charge ignored me, ordering his guards to seize the man I had fallen on. As four guards dragged the strange man away, I got my first look at his face. It was not pretty; his dark features were screwed into a scowl. He gave me a look of utter contempt and spat at me. I skipped a couple of paces backward, just in time to avoid the glob of brown spittle.

The Tyrant takes aim

Turning to me, the officer bowed and motioned for me to follow him. He led me to the emperor's carriage with the remaining pike men forming an honor guard. He stopped twenty feet from the carriage and announced, "His majesty, Charles V." Nothing in Army basic training had prepared me to meet a sixteenth century ruler, so instinct took over; I prostrated myself before the gilded carriage, my monk's cassock splayed out on the stony path.

Charles V, Holy Roman Emperor, rose from his seat, smiled, and said, "Thank you for saving my life, Friar."

So, Alex, that's how I met Charles V, Emperor of the Holy Roman Empire, in the year 1522. One minute, I was gawking at the Emperor's procession from my perch in a scraggy oak tree, and the next, the King invited me to join him in his royal carriage.

The carriage soon arrived at the entrance to the imperial castle, high above the city of Nürnberg. The Emperor's guards treated me with almost as much respect as they did Charles, for I had (unwittingly) saved his life. As a lowly G.I., I was unaccustomed to such deference by high-ranking military officers. Checking a salute, my conditioned response to anyone with insignia on his shoulders, I accepted the commander's proffered hand and stepped down from the carriage. When the great stone doors of the castle swung open, Charles V and his retinue entered, and I followed a respectful ten paces behind.

Wandering the old city of Nürnberg as a twentieth-century G.I., I had often seen this castle from the outside. The castle hill, with its commanding view of the oldest part of the walled city was popular with residents and visitors to Nürnberg. I recalled taking a snapshot from this vantage point with my Brownie camera—snow covered peaked roofs poking through the fog.

Here is that photograph, Alex. Black and white film captured the dreamlike scene, and it still looks good, forty years later. The boulders in the foreground are part of the natural hill, and you can see the road leading up hill to the castle—the same road I traveled with Charles V.

Once, with a group of tourists, I heard the story, probably invented for Americans, that the nursery rhyme, "Jack and Jill," was based on

Nürnberg history. Supposedly, a couple accused of adultery was yoked together and forced to walk up the steep path. As often as not, the man or woman would slip, causing the pair to "come tumbling down." The tour guide also pointed to that boulder—right there, Alex—and claimed that horses' hooves made the indentions in it when they leapt from the castle, their riders fleeing the king's guards. Do you see that tall house on the open square? It belonged to Albrecht Dürer, a famous Nürnberg artist who lived during the time my adventure took place. Let me tell you, Alex; it felt eerie to be in a familiar place five hundred years before I had first become acquainted with it.

Standing before the emperor, disguised as a monk, I had little time to reflect on my circumstances. I was acutely aware that one wrong move on my part could be fatal. If the king suspected that I was a foreigner, an alien from another time, he could order my immediate execution—or worse. My earlier encounter with the *Scharfrichter* made me all too aware of the ingenious forms of punishment at his disposal. Danger has a way of honing one's senses to a razor edge. Every word from Charles V, and the slightest movements of his facial features, were signals—emergency flares—as clear to me as a touchdown run on your big screen TV.

Fortunately for me, the city fathers observed strict protocol for the reception of the Holy Roman Emperor. As an honored but unofficial guest, I was allowed to observe from the sidelines. This enabled me to decipher the hierarchy of the king's attendants and the Nürnberg officials and to learn the proper diplomatic etiquette. This knowledge would be invaluable—perhaps lifesaving—if I were to survive as an ersatz monk in the emperor's court.

Charles seemed bored by the ceremony and cut it short with the announcement that he was tired from his long journey to Nürnberg. Princes, bishops, margraves, and other officials representing the patchwork of kingdoms, principalities, and free imperial cities comprising the Holy Roman Empire had been arriving in Nürnberg for weeks. The Diet of 1522 would convene the following day. As members of the welcoming committee departed, imperial guards escorted Charles to his quarters. The king turned to see me lurking in the shadows, hoping to make my escape. "Come with me, Friar," he said.

When the king and I entered his chambers, and the guards closed the heavy, stone door, I was filled with dread. This was it—the moment of truth, when Charles would discover my true identity, and I would be burned at the city gate. I had not been so frightened since basic training, when Sergeant Miller gave me that "lesson in marksmanship" at the firing range. Crouched in a foxhole with my M-1 rifle, I had done my best to attain a "tight shot group"—all of my bullets striking the target in the same, small area. Apparently, Sergeant Miller did not think my best was good enough.

"Tighten up that shot group, boy," he had shouted, punctuating his words by pounding on my helmet with a steel ammunition box. When that instructional technique failed to improve my aim, he yanked me from my foxhole and dragged me to a latrine constructed of masonry blocks, commonly known as a "brick shit house." I knew I was in trouble when Sergeant Miller ejected the only other occupant of the building in the middle of his business and closed the door.

Now, alone with the Holy Roman Emperor, I recalled that incident. The symptoms were the same: knocking knees, shortness of breath, profuse sweating, and a desperate attempt to remember the prayers I had learned in Sunday school.

"You can relax, Bob; I'm not going to stuff you down the commode, as Sergeant Miller threatened to do."

Here we go again, I thought, another character in this schizoid dream, or whatever it is, who seems to know all about me.

"More to the point, Bob, you are here to learn about me. Our mutual friend, Monk, sent you 'out on a limb,' so to speak, to ensure that we would have some one-on-one, quality time together."

"Your Highness…" I began.

"Call me Chuck."

"Uh, Chuck," I gulped, "You know Monk?"

"Sure, Bob, Monk and I are old buds. But, you know, I really am getting tired, and I have to deal with all those politicians tomorrow. Let's get down to business."

"Business?"

"Soul business, Bob. By now you have a pretty good idea why Monk pulled you out of that long dark night of your soul and brought you to this place and time."

"You mean that pitch black tunnel where I spent Christmas Eve hiding from those drunken G.I.s?"

"Yes, Bob. You learned about the *fight or flight* reaction to stress. You demonstrated a capacity to fight when the first guy burst into your squad room, but your choice to flee when the rest of his platoon followed, bent on turning you into a Christmas pudding, made sense. You had some acquaintance with your inner Warrior and the beginning of your Magician wisdom."

"Apparently not enough, Chuck. My apprenticeships with the Scharfrichter and Hans Behaim made me aware the difference between a boy and a man."

"Well, that's why you're here, Bob. Your *'four mighty ones,'* as Blake called them, happen to be here in sixteenth-century Nürnberg, to initiate you into manhood."

"Monk called them: Warrior, Magician, King, and Lover."

"As will Robert Moore and Douglas Gillette," but I'm getting ahead of myself."

"I thought I knew something about the Warrior, being a soldier and all…"

"But you learned from the Scharfrichter, the city hangman, that the Warrior is more than fighting and heroics."

"Yeah, I mean yes, Your Highness, er, Chuck, the Scharfrichter taught me that courage means doing one's duty, no matter how hard it is. Later, Monk and I had a long talk about courage. He told me that a real man has to have courage to do the right thing, whether it's a paramedic struggling to aid a resisting victim or a husband sharing his true feelings with his wife."

"Not exactly the superhero image from comics books, huh Bob?"

"No, I guess it takes a lot to be a man…"

"A real man."

"Yes sir."

"And what did you learn from Hans Behaim?"

"The architect? The secret of his magic was a combination of curiosity, commitment, and courage. Scientists, engineers, intellectuals—all kind of magicians—have to be curious about the world, asking the right questions and committed to a lifetime of study. And they have to have the courage to expose their ideas to the world."

"There's that word again, Bob—courage."

"I learned from Hans Behaim that it takes guts to tackle a new skill. It would have been easy for him to say, 'I can't do math,' when he was ordered to build a hospital that would withstand the current of the Pegnitz river, or 'I don't want to upset my colleague,' when he was told to modify the design of the *Kornhaus*. It takes real courage to overcome the fear of failure. Now that you mention it, Chuck, how come both the hangman and the architect emphasized courage? Isn't that redundant?"

"You will learn, Bob, that the Warrior, Magician, King, and Lover work together inside of you. Each has a different function, but we share certain traits. As your King, I must be Warrior, Magician, Lover, and more—your father."

My father. I thought of my own father—a shadowy, inaccessible member of my birth family, bully one moment and victim the next. Pacing the floor of that South Side shack we called home in his boxer shorts, sipping his wine or beer, watching the fights on television, he rarely spoke. I remember only one word—"MIND!" accompanied by a swat at me. From my father, I learned to duck—to duck out of the house when he and my mother fought, to duck out of any confrontation, and to duck out of honest communication of feelings. What could my King teach me about fatherhood?

Charles V, Holy Roman Emperor, once again read my mind. Putting an arm around my shoulder, he said, "Bob my boy, we have a lot of soul work to do and only a short time to do it. During my stay in Nürnberg, you shall accompany me to all Diet functions. In your monk's cassock, you may observe in silence my actions and words. At vespers, you and I shall retire to this place before the hearth, where you shall learn the secrets of your own King and father."

I don't mind telling you, Alex, as I lay in my featherbed and tried to get to sleep that night, I wept.

* * *

Sounds from the King's chambers awakened me; it was morning, and Charles was moving about. A common fireplace made it possible for me to hear him from my own room, despite the thick, stone walls separating us. When I crouched low, I could also catch an occasional glimpse of him through the smoke and flames. He seemed to be pacing the floor and chanting something.

There was a knock at the door of his room. "Enter," said Charles. Several men, apparently servants, came in with a tray of breakfast, garments, and toiletries for the King's ablutions. Charles took all this—apparently a daily routine—in stride, joking and addressing each man by name. They, in turn, ordered him to raise his arms, turn this way and that, and step into his royal garments. My impression was that the King and his servants were a team, preparing a presentation—an image—worthy of the Holy Roman Empire. It was as though the King were serving his people, not the other way around.

I thought about good leaders I had observed in my brief military experience. When Colonel Clay inspected his regiment, the Second Armored Cavalry, his boots were more highly polished, his uniform more perfectly pressed, his brass shinier, than those of any soldier before him. By his appearance and bearing, he presented an example for his troops to emulate. He held himself to the highest standard, so that the hours we spent spit-shining our boots were honorable, not onerous. In like manner, Charles V, Emperor of the Holy Roman Empire, demonstrated that an effective leader takes his image seriously, because it is part of his responsibility to his people. Moreover, the King—"Chuck"—taught me that a leader's image is not the same as the leader himself. He must not confuse the two or take himself too seriously. He respects and serves his servants as much as they respect and serve him.

I donned my monk's cassock and waited in the Emperor's antechamber. Charles soon appeared. He winked at me, asking, "hungry?"

"I sure am, Chuck," I said.

"Remember yourself Friar" the King responded, "what's said in my chambers stays in my chambers. In public, it's 'your royal highness' please."

"Yes your royal highness," I answered softly, folding my hands and lowering my eyes under the hood of my cassock.

I followed Charles to a kitchen of sorts, where he indicated that I was to join the castle staff for breakfast. "Return to my antechamber when you are finished, Friar. It will soon be time for the opening procession."

The breads and tea were, if not fit for a king, then certainly fit for a king's retinue. I was grateful for the barrier of my monk's getup. Were it not for my presumed veil of silence, I would have been expected to banter with the others, chatting in rapid-fire street slang. I would have been like "Schatzie," the German lady who sold the *Stars and Stripes* newspaper in the mess hall. Regardless of whatever smart-aleck remark addressed to her in G.I. slang, she simply took the money and replied, *"Morgan, Schatzie."*

Back in the King's antechamber, I waited alone until a fanfare of trumpets from somewhere in the imperial castle announced the opening of the 1522 Diet of the Holy Roman Empire. Charles and his attendants entered the antechamber. I took my position, ten paces behind the King, and the heavy door to the Great Hall swung open. Flanked by imperial guards, we marched into a cavernous room dominated by a great table shaped like a cross, but with extra crossbars to provide seating for the princes, bishops, margraves, and other leaders representing every principality and free imperial city in the empire. Behind each chair stood the attendants of that leader. Those leaders positioned closer to the head of the cross seemed to have more attendants than did those at the base. As the trumpets played, Charles V took his seat at the head of the cross, facing all the others. His guards, attendants, and I stood behind the King. The other dignitaries then took their seats. Charles announced that the Diet had begun.

The meeting dragged on forever, Alex. It would have made you think of a boring day in school, with summer vacation just around the corner.

All through the morning, one prince, *Bürgermeister*, bishop, or margrave after another rose to praise Charles V. As Chuck explained later, these "encomia," as he called them, were all part of the show.

You probably have kids like that in your classes, Alex—"brown-nosers," we used to call them.

I knew from reading about such toadies in the *Chicago Tribune*, that these politicians were jockeying for position in the real business of this diet that would follow the mid-day meal. They were just like aldermen in the city council, currying favor with Mayor Daley that would translate into future clout.

After a sumptuous meal—fish, venison, and pork, washed down with barrels of wine—Charles demonstrated his leadership, giving each leader a chance to present his case. At issue were territorial disputes within the empire, external threats, especially from the Moslem Empire, relations with the Pope, and the emerging threat posed by Martin Luther and his followers. Chuck listened to each man, asking questions to ensure his own understanding, and acknowledging each speaker with a brief summary. At the time, I was puzzled, because his style was so different from that of my teachers in high school or instructors in the military, who always seemed more interested in control than in communication. Looking back now, from the twenty-first century, I'm convinced that the King was channeling Stephen Covey: "Seek first to understand, then to be understood." I was impressed that the assorted politicians responded to Chuck's leadership style. At one point, some guy—I think he was the Bishop of Bamberg—tried to filibuster, but Charles broke in, "You have made an excellent case, Herr Bishop. Let us hear what others have to say in response." Everyone seemed to catch on; they realized that they would each get more attention if they stated their main points clearly and succinctly, and then listened for feedback. At the same time, they understood that Charles was the emperor, and he was their best hope for peace and prosperity.

At the end of the first day, following another huge meal, Chuck and I retired to his chamber. I was as happy to get out of my monk's getup as he was to hang up his robes and crown. He dismissed the servants, and we relaxed before the fire. "So now you've seen your first diet of the Holy Roman Empire, Bob, what do you think?"

I told him that I was impressed with his restrained use of raw power. "You maintained control of that bunch of ambitious politicians by 'empowering' them, as we learned to say in the twentieth century."

"Yes, but it's not as easy as it looks. When giving a man the power to speak, one must earn the right to reclaim control by listening to the man."

"So listening is not a passive act..."

"Quite the contrary, Bob; active listening requires a large expenditure of energy to understand the speaker's words—and the way they are spoken, and to read the speaker's nonverbal cues."

"So that bishop from Bamberg…"

"Herr Bishop Georg III Schenk von Limpurg"

"Yeah…When he went on and on about that alliance…"

"The *Schmalkaldic League*"

"Right, well it seemed kind of boring to me, but you didn't cut him off right away."

"No, he has some good insights about the religious problems brewing here in Germany, so I waited until he started repeating himself. Some people just like the sound of their own voice. If I had let him drone on, the other delegates would have dozed off, and we would have lost the value of their perspectives."

"So, it's like they would see the same problem, but in different ways?"

"Sure, Bob, a bishop is going to see Luther's ideas as a threat to the church's authority, but a prince might view them as evidence of critical thinking. Peasants might question the right of princes to tax their labor."

"So who's right?"

"The truth is, Bob, they're all right, or at least, partly right. Your eyes are like a window on the world. They are connected to your brain which holds the sum total of your experience—everything you know to be true. If you are a farmer, you may look through the window of your barn and see a cow. To you, that cow is an animal; you pulled it from its mother's womb. You feed it. You shovel its manure. You milk it. You will one day sell it. A *Hausfrau* sees the cow as meat in the butcher shop—a meal for her family. A lord, passing the peasant's farm in his carriage, counts the cow as a source of revenue. The same cow is indeed, something different to each pair of eyes. A King's job is to understand His subjects and enable them to passionately give their talents to build a kingdom that fulfills all of their needs and aspirations."

"Tough job."

"Yes, well, it's easier said than done. For instance, when I first took over Castile, you could say I screwed up royally."

"Oh yeah?"

"I'm embarrassed to even talk about it, Bob. You should have seen me—Mr. Bigshot—putting all my own guys in office…"

"Kind of like Chicago politicians handing out patronage jobs…"

"In a way, yes, but ward politics is built on doing favors for people: getting a sidewalk fixed or getting a tree cut down—making everyone feel like an insider, a part of the system. My mistake in Spain was to do a lot of taking without giving much back. They didn't much like me."

"I hope this doesn't sound rude, Chuck, seeing as how you could have my head chopped off with a snap of your fingers, but how come the Mentor sent me to you for instruction?"

The emperor laughed so hard he cried. "Bob my boy, let's make one thing clear: I represent King energy, but just like the Scharfrichter and Hans Behaim, I'm a real person. You are going to take what you learn from us and do the best you can with it, but you'll screw up too. We're working the tension here, between an ideal and its dark side—the Shadow."

"Oh yeah, I think I encountered some shadowy figures before. That "Lion" guy had a Warrior's ferocity, but he seemed to enjoy being cruel. His boss, the Scharfrichter, used His Warrior energy only to serve a higher good. And that creepy guy working at the hospital was pretty smart, I guess, but he tried to recruit me to sabotage the architect's plan."

"Okay Bob, so you know that, as the King, I represent power, but that energy can be used for good or for evil. As a mere mortal, I find it a real struggle to maintain the high ground. But I am going to ask your help. To accomplish the task I shall set before you, you must call upon your Warrior and your Magician. If you are successful, you will find your own King within."

"Does this involve violence? I'm a little squeamish about violence."

"Maybe."

"Great... And I suppose this task is going to be a bit more mentally challenging than K.P. and walking my post in a military manner, keeping always on the alert and observing everything within sight or hearing?"

"A bit. By the way, was that you sleeping in the cab of the deuce-and-a-half out at the air strip last week?"

"You've been talking to Mentor, Chuck. I can't seem to get away with anything in this trip down the Collective Memory Lane."

"We have all been watching and waiting for you, Bob. It's not every day that we get the chance to turn a chickenshit, clueless, kid with a hard-on into something resembling a man."

"Thanks for the build-up, Chuck, so what's this task you guys have in mind for me?"

"Okay, Bob, listen up. Remember that guy who tried to assassinate me on the road to this castle?"

"Oh sure, the weirdo. I sure saved your royal butt, didn't I?"

"It's fortunate for both of us that your head was thicker than the branch you were sitting on. Anyway, that guy has been dogging me ever since I was old enough to take on this job. Being king of an empire stretching from Luxembourg to Castile to Austria, it's easy to get a big head. As I mentioned earlier, I sometimes screw up. When I do, that guy always seems to be around. Your mission, should you choose to accept it, is to learn what you can about him, track him down, and arrest him."

CHAPTER NINE

Pursuit of a Tyrant

So, Alex, where would you look for a would-be assassin in a strange country, five hundred years before your own time? I did not know either, but it was clear to me that I had no choice; if I did not catch him, I would never get home to my sweetheart.

Armed only with the emperor's amulet—a sort of good luck charm about the size of a quarter, with religious symbols —I left the castle by a side door in the servants' quarters. Looking down over the city and the road traveled by Charles and his procession, I spotted the tree from which I had fallen on the angry man who had tried to kill the emperor. I remembered how big the man was, and the skillful way he had handled his weapon. I remembered the man's piercing black eyes—the way they had fixed me when I inadvertently foiled the assassination attempt. It occurred to me at that moment to make my way back to Mentor and negotiate with Him for an easy way out of this frightening mission.

Then I thought about Gerdi, and something inside—my Warrior perhaps—told me that I had to do this; fear would have to be set aside for the moment. "Keep your mind on the mission," the voice said, "and do what you have to do."

I stared blankly at the spindly oak tree, at a loss for a plan. As a G.I., I had been trained for a military occupational specialty—radio operator— and undergone training in military basics: first aid, map reading, weapons, and "military bearing"—the "how-to" skills I would need as a soldier. However, as a lowly ranking enlisted man, the Army had taught me only one decision-making rule: "Obey the last order first!" Now I was faced with a challenge requiring high-level thinking. Where to start?

I recalled my apprenticeship with Hans Behaim, a man who had studied his entire life to unlock his magical skills in architecture and problem solving. During one of our late-night sessions before the crackling fireplace, Herr Behaim had advised me: "When faced with a problem, remain calm and optimistic; there is always a solution." That thought comforted me. But what had the great man said about solving problems, such as the construction of the *Kornhaus* grain storage facility, using an earlier city wall for its foundation? "Define the problem—list everything you know about it. Set some boundaries to keep your vision—the goal—in focus."

I paced back and forth on the castle hillside, trying to remember details of my encounter with the assassin. I pictured the man: stalwart, swarthy, intense, simple attire—and his expression of utter contempt when I fell onto him, deflecting his arrow. What else? Oh yes—the large man's brutal disregard for spectators clinging to the hillside as he disappeared into the crowd. The disturbing image of women and children being shoved from boulders, landing in a heap on the rocky ground, made it difficult for me to remember the direction taken by the man. What sort of person would have such hatred for his king and so little regard for his fellow citizens?

That sort of person—a Tyrant—might stand out in the crowd, I reasoned. His behavior would contrast with that of the majority of Nürnbergers—citizens who respect one another and their "shining city on the hill."

"The first part of my problem—to find the Tyrant—might be a matter of mingling with the people, observing, and listening for reports of an uncivil stranger. But the second part of my problem was more daunting," I thought. "What would I do if I found the Tyrant?" The words of Hans Behaim came back to me:

"Make a list of ideas, anything that comes into your head. Don't worry if some ideas seem silly or irrelevant while you are making this list. As you write each idea, make new associations, and write them down. Let your mind play! You will be amazed at the variety of approaches to your problem."

So I called upon my inner Magician to brainstorm ideas: challenge him to a duel, catch him by surprise, garrote him with a rope from behind, assemble a posse to take him by force, show him my G.I. uniform and speak modern English to frighten him, command him in the name of the Emperor to accompany me, trick him into thinking that I would help him assassinate the Emperor, poison him…. Herr Behaim's advice had been correct; I was impressed with the variety of my own ideas. So it was not hopeless, I thought, there is a solution!

I then switched my mode of thinking from generating solutions to eliminating ideas that would not serve my mission. I was supposed to arrest the Tyrant, not kill him; garroting or poisoning him were not options. Revealing my own true identity and trying to recruit a posse were too risky, as they would require people to believe the unbelievable. My best bet was to "fight fire with fire," using the Shadow-side Trickster aspect of my own Magician to lure the Tyrant to the presence of the King.

With the outline of a plan in mind, I walked down the castle hill toward the main marketplace. Perhaps the Tyrant had created a wake of upset citizens in that great sea of merchants, artisans, and shoppers.

The first clue as to the Tyrant's whereabouts was a bawling old woman flower vendor. She complained loudly, to no one in particular, that a big brute of a man, a stranger, had forced her to arrange a bouquet of her prettiest flowers just for him. He then berated her because she asked for a premium of only one *Heller*, upset her flower cart, and stalked off without buying the bouquet after all. I, the silent monk, helped the old woman right her cart and then followed the Tyrant's trail south, the direction in which she indicated he had gone.

As I crossed the Pegnitz, I looked to my left, where renovation of the hospital was progressing nicely, and thought fondly of Hans Behaim, the architect who had awakened the Magician within my soul. I looked to my right, toward the hangman's bridge, and thanked the *Scharfrichter* for teaching me the meaning of courage—doing what must be done, in spite of my own fear. I knew that my confrontation with the Tyrant would be a test of my mental agility, my bravery, and the leadership principles I had observed in the King: serve the common good.

A commotion in *Königstraße*, near St. Lorenz Church, drew my attention. A merchant selling practical items—what we would call hardware—was sitting next to his cart wiping blood from his forehead. From what I could gather, a man answering to the description of the Tyrant had set upon the vendor. The man had picked up a sturdy coil of rope and a hatchet as if to purchase them. When the merchant leaned forward to accept payment, the brutish stranger had struck him with the rope and run off.

I wondered what the Tyrant would do with rope and a hatchet. Nothing good, I concluded, as I continued south, toward the *Frauentor*, or Ladies Gate, where the Emperor had entered the walled city from the south. When I reached the Frauentor, I immediately perceived an answer to my own question.

When the emperor's entourage departed Nürnberg via the Frauentor, as it surely would, it would have to negotiate a zigzag course through twin doors, drop gates with bronze spikes, an inner wall, and an outer wall before reaching the drawbridge. This obstacle course was designed, of course, to slow an assault upon the city. It could also be integral to the Tyrant's nefarious scheme to overthrow Emperor Charles V. At some point, the emperor's carriage would be cut off from his guards. Could the Tyrant be planning to cut the rope holding the drop gate, trapping the king? But what about the driver and guard on the emperor's carriage? Studying the infrastructure of the gate, I could see places where the Tyrant could hide as the main contingent of guards passed, cut the drop gate rope, and then use his stolen rope to swing down like Tarzan, catching Charles and his men by surprise. The Tyrant was smart, strong, and ruthless enough to carry off such a plan.

But why? Pure hatred? Maybe. After all, he might have been apprehended after his castle hill assassination attempt. Yet, he did escape the highly trained and motivated emperor's guards. Perhaps he chose that spot with his escape route in mind. Could the Tyrant have a plan to seize power from Charles V?

As I studied the Frauentor and thought about the Tyrant's possible motivation, something behind me cast a shadow on the cobblestone street. Powerful hands gripped my shoulders and spun me around—the Tyrant!

"You think you have it all figured out, don't you, Bob?"

"How do you know my...oh, you're one of *them*."

"That's right, you miserable little creep, I'm your worst nightmare—that part of you that will get carried away with any authority you might be given. I'm your acting sergeant, your petty bureaucrat, your unreasonable boss, and your little corporal—Napoleon or Hitler. You're going to have to fight me the rest of your life, so you had better start right now."

I thrust the emperor's amulet in the Tyrant's face. "In the name of Charles V, Holy Roman Emperor, I command you to bow before me!"

The Tyrant threw his ugly head back and roared with laughter. "I'm winning already," he said. "You think you can command my respect with sheer authority? That's my game."

I thought of my own platoon sergeant, a nasty little man who could only intimidate lower-ranking members of his unit with his stripes. His attempts to suck up to fellow noncoms and officers were met with thinly disguised contempt.

I changed my tact: "Sir, I apologize. You are far too clever for a lowly young soldier such as I. Would you consider rapprochement with the King, for the good of your subjects?"

At my words of appeasement, the Tyrant assumed an arrogant demeanor. He turned his back, making me wait. Finally, still looking away from me, he announced, "Charles will meet with me, in this very spot, at midnight tonight. He must walk from the castle to the Frauntor unaccompanied by his guards or anyone else except you. And he must be attired in his vestments and crown."

The ludicrous image of Charles V, Holy Roman Emperor, hiking down castle hill, through the main marketplace, across the river, and into this trap set for him by the Tyrant, set my mind reeling. My plan of tricking the Tyrant into coming to the Imperial castle and being taken into custody by the royal guards had seemingly backfired. I realized, to my chagrin, that my own Trickster was no match for that of the Tyrant. My mission was in jeopardy; I might never return to Gerdi and my own time.

Then the words of Hans Behaim, master architect, archetype of my own Magician, with its quest for knowledge and its critical thinking energy, appeared in a cartoon bubble over the Tyrant's head: "Never give up! There is always a solution."

"As you command, sir," I replied in my most obsequious tone. "How shall I arrange…"

"Details! Handle it, boy!" commanded the Tyrant. "Now be gone! I have important work to do."

I retreated, keeping an eye on the Tyrant as long as possible. The sinister fellow disappeared inside the Frauentor—undoubtedly attending to his murderous machinations. I hurried to the castle, dreading the message I must deliver to Chuck.

CHAPTER TEN

Triumph of the King

Nürnberg was in a festive mood. The Diet of 1522 had come to a close. Delegates were celebrating their political victories and toasting alliances in the city's pubs. The citizenry joined in, congratulating one another on their successful hospitality of Charles V, beloved emperor.

In Charles' private chambers at the castle, I related the Tyrant's demand. "I am so sorry, Your Highness, that I was not able to lure the would-be assassin to the royal dungeon."

"There is greater risk, meeting the Tyrant on His own terms, Bob, but you did find Him and arrange for Him to meet me. You have succeeded far beyond your own expectations. And it's Chuck, remember?"

"Huh?"

The King motioned for me to be seated. "Son, to free my people of His tyranny, I shall gladly take the risk of entering The Dark One's lair."

"But Charles, er, Chuck! He has an ax…and rope! I'm sure he wants to kill you and don your royal garments to assume the throne!"

"Of course, Bob, but he is not so very clever as he thinks."

"Pardon my saying this, Chuck, but he seems to have the Magician's zeal for planning, the Warrior's ability to fight, and Your own will to lead. He's pretty scary!"

"Yes, Bob, but look; the Tyrant has all the weaklings on his side: The Magician's Trickster, the Warrior's Sadist, as well as that unfortunate potential in my own personality, the Tyrant. In the fullness of my King, I have the pure energies of the Magician and the Warrior to back me up. I am also powered by love for my people."

"Love? What's love got to do with it?"

"Only everything, Bob," said the emperor. "What is this entire quest of yours about?"

"Getting back to Gerdi…oh…I see what you're saying, Chuck."

"Exactly! It's no accident that Monk, your Mentor, arranged for you to encounter your Warrior, Magician, and King energies before you meet your Lover. Without us, you couldn't handle the power of love."

"So if you're all about the King, leadership and all…"

"Then I must be powered by love—love for my people. Sheer power, without love, is…"

"The Tyrant!"

"Yes."

"So, Chuck, why is it so important to capture the Tyrant?"

"I must confess Bob, that like everyone who comes into power, I have been tempted to abuse it. At times I have succumbed to that temptation."

"Really?"

"Oh yes. Just ask the good folks of Castile; they were not happy with me when I came in there with my own guys, playing the big shot, and sticking them with the bills for my ambitious military adventures. The Tyrant got hold of me. If I am to redeem myself, I must get Him under control."

"So what's the plan, Chuck? You gonna meet him tonight in His *Frauentor* trap all alone and whip his ass?"

"Not exactly, Bob. I know myself well enough to realize that my Tyrant could win unless I have help from the people I serve."

"The people you serve? I thought everyone hereabouts serves you."

"It's a two-way street, as you say in your time. When I am at my best, I am what folks will one day call a 'servant-leader.' I serve and protect my people, and they will go to the ropes for me."

"*Serve and protect;* that's a catchy phrase. They should paint that on police cars."

"You'll have to check with Mentor on that, Bob, I have enough to keep me busy here in the sixteenth century."

"'Go to the ropes'…?"

"Yeah, well, Mentor is a fight fan, and we sometimes stray from the agenda in our weekly team meetings…"

"Okay, Chuck, let's get back to *our* agenda. You're saying that you'll have help tonight?"

"Yes. Remember, people do for tyrants only what they are forced to.

When push comes to shove, tyrants are alone. That includes Tyrant. He will try to trick me into a vulnerable position and overpower me. But he will get a surprise."

"Your people?"

"Yes."

"You trust them with your life?"

"Yes."

"This I gotta see!"

When the bells of *St. Sebaldus* announced 2300 hours, and the night watchmen had made their rounds in each quarter of Nürnberg, closing pubs and sending revelers home, Charles V, in full regalia, sallied forth from His imperial fortress to meet His fate in the dark maze of stone and needle-sharp drop gates that was the *Frauntor*. A once frightened, ignorant, weak, G.I. now armed with Warrior's courage, Magician's mental acuity, and King's power, accompanied Charles on the cross-town hike. They were an incongruous pair in the empty streets. What was that black form in the lamplight? Were those the sounds of rats scurrying across the marketplace—or footsteps? Were the eyes peering down at them connected to a shadowy being or to saints carved into the stone of *St. Lorenz*? They strode on to the Frauentor.

Minutes before midnight, with the little convent church of St. Martha on their left and St. Clara's convent on their right, they faced the double doors leading to the Frauntor. I shuttered, remembering the drop gates just beyond, where I was sure Tyrant would make His move. Would He cut the rope holding the drop gate with his ax, impaling them on the razor-sharp spikes? Would He allow them to pass through the gate before sending it crashing down, trapping them? Perhaps He would use the distraction to decapitate them with His ax. I tried to consider all the possibilities and counter-measures I could take to defend the King.

A dark figure leapt from the six-foot stone wall surrounding St. Clara's convent, landing directly behind them—the Tyrant! I spun around to see Him advancing, ax in hand, like the predator He was.

"The great King, led by His Judas goat, reports to me as ordered! Step lively now, or I'll whack your heads off!"

Charles calmly walked under the drop gate, into the confinement of the Frauntor's labyrinth. I followed on shaky legs, humming "Nearer my God to Thee." As I had feared, the Tyrant swung his ax as soon as the three of them were past the drop gate, cutting its rope. The massive slab of iron smashed the cobblestone street, splattering stone fragments on the trio. I noticed then, for the first time, that a spool of heavy chain recessed in the city wall, had been stretched across the passageway ahead. The Tyrant had carefully set a trap for us, and now he would pounce, like a tomcat on his prey.

"Off with the crown, Charles! Off with the robe!"

"I think not, Tyrant," replied the King calmly. "There was a time when I would have been swayed by your methods, but my Warrior and my Magician have taught me a better way, and my Lover has made me a better man. You no longer have power over me."

"I got my power right here," growled Tyrant, shifting his ax from one hand to the other like a knife-wielding juvenile delinquent in a 1950s teen drama.

"And I get my power from the people I serve," said the King, motioning to his elite guards, who moved from the shadowy recesses of the Frauntor.

I realized then that the King had been in control of the encounter all along, sending his guards to the Frauentor via the broad ramparts of the wall surrounding Nürnberg. They had positioned themselves to protect the King, from the Tyrant, even as He was spying on our every movement as we made our way from the castle to the Frauentor. The emperor's Warrior had overcome His fear; His Magician had devised a plan, and His Lover had bestowed upon Him the fierce devotion of his protectors.

As the emperor's guards led the Tyrant off in chains, Charles turned to me. We walked through the city gate and across a drawbridge over the moat surrounding the walled city. We walked into the clearing beyond and turned around at the *Scharfrichter's* gallows. The roofs of the moonlit city spread before us, climbing to the heights of the imperial castle. "I leave Nürnberg in the morning, Bob. I leave my people stronger and better able to govern themselves."

"You will remain with me forever, Chuck."

We walked back to the oldest part of town, through the crooked streets below the imperial castle, talking about the responsibilities, challenges, and rewards of the King. Charles V, Holy Roman Emperor, shook my hand and bid me *auf wiedersehen* before we parted. Charles walked up castle hill, returning to His life of service to the people. I made my way to Mentor's hole in the wall.

CHAPTER ELEVEN

The King Within

I pushed the heavy, wooden door and stumbled into Monk's chamber, causing Him to stir.

"Do you know what time it is young man?"

"Yeah," I replied, "you gotta hear what happened tonight!"

"Later, Bob, I'm grumpy when I don't get my forty winks."

"Oh, sorry, Monk, good night."

"Good night!"

I tried to sleep, but the events surrounding my meeting with Charles, the Diet, and the King's triumph over Tyrant kept me awake until dawn. When the first rays of sunlight shone through the tiny windows of Monk's room, I heard the popping of boiling water. A few minutes later, Monk's too-cheery voice announced breakfast.

I accepted the steaming cup of tea and hunk of black bread with gratitude. It was a welcome change from the rich fare I had enjoyed at the castle. Although I was exhausted from lack of sleep, I felt at ease with Mentor and eager to share my latest experience.

"So, Bob, what did you learn from your King?"

"Well, He has a lot of power, and His decisions affect the lives of people throughout Europe. That's one thing. Another thing is, all that power can go to His head. He told me about some mistakes He made when He first took over Spain—playing the big shot, pushing people around, that sort of thing."

"Anything like that ever happen to you, Bob?"

"Are you kidding? I've never been anyone's boss."

"What about that door-to-door sales business you and Kash ran when you were in high school? You had employees then."

"Hmm…that's true, Mentor. I guess I didn't think of them so much as employees as customers. After all, we didn't make any money unless they did."

"Interesting! What might Emperor Charles V say about that?"

"He was fond of saying that His power came from the people. They would take care of Him if He took care of them." I then related the story of Tyrant's capture and the role Charles' men played.

"Those guys went out in the middle of the night, not knowing what to expect or what tricks Tyrant might have up His sleeve. They were glad to do it though, because they knew that Charles would do the same for them. He called Himself a 'Servant Leader.' He might say that by teaching those kids everything we knew about selling and giving them the support they needed, we were serving them. They in turn worked hard to sell, making our efforts pay off."

"Did it always work?"

"Not always. Sometimes we would catch a kid loafing, instead of selling."

"What happened then?"

"Kash would get mad and yell, 'You're fired!' "

"And what did you do?"

"I would hire the kid back. We were not paying the boys by the hour, and we only made money when we had salesmen out on the street."

"Mr. Nice Guy, huh?"

"Well, yeah."

"What do you think a kid would learn from that experience?"

"Oh, I think I know what you are saying, Mentor; I was teaching the kid that rules and discipline don't matter."

"Doing him a big favor, huh?"

"No, I guess not."

"What would the King have done?"

"I think the King would have asked questions and listened to the answers. He is a great listener. He might have adjusted the rules to accommodate the needs of employees when appropriate, to help them sell more. At other times, He might have communicated His expectations clearly and given the kid some much-needed discipline."

"Okay, so you learned that the King cares about His people; He gives them what they need to do the job. He listens to them. Sometimes He lays down the law. Anything else?"

"Yes—definitely. The King has the other two guys working with Him—the Warrior and the Magician."

"Really?"

"Well, for instance, His Warrior helps Him to do what He has to do, whether it's taking charge of a meeting of egotistical, petty rulers or leading an army into battle."

"And His Magician?"

"He has to be able to plan and manage infrastructure to unite his empire, He has to understand the people and politics of groups within the empire and outside of it. He has to outsmart His enemies, including His own Tyrant. All that takes a lifelong commitment to study, deep reflection, creativity, and critical thinking—the mark of the Magician."

"Bob, you are learning your lessons well—the reason you were brought here. But you have one more apprenticeship—a big one."

"Just one more? Then I can get back home to the twentieth century—and Gerdi?"

"That's right, Bob."

"Who is it?"

"Maybe you can guess, Bob. What do you suppose motivated Charles V to lead His people, to listen to them, to learn from His mistakes, to risk His own life for them?"

"There's only one force strong enough, Mentor, the same force urging me on through this crazy journey—love. All I want is to get back to my Gerdi."

"Bingo! But are you prepared for love?"

"Prepared? I have to be prepared?"

"I'm afraid so, Bob, and I know just the guy to teach you about your Lover. How's your penmanship?"

"My penmanship? Not great, Mentor, what do you have in store for me?"

"You have one more apprenticeship here in sixteenth century Nürnberg, Bob, scribe to the great *Meistersinger*, Hans Sachs."

"I think I've heard of him. Wasn't he in an opera by Richard Wagner?"

"The very same guy. He writes poetry too—the kind that your oh-so-serious, black-clad Poetry 101 teacher will dismiss as doggerel, but it contains simple truths about life. As you transcribe his verses, think about their implication for your own Lover."

Hans Sachs, Meistersinger

Chapter Twelve

The Lover

Here's where things get really interesting, Alex!

Following Monk's directions, I approached the main marketplace. Now that the Diet of 1522 was over, the good citizens of Nürnberg were restoring their city to normal—removing the wooden structures erected for viewing the emperor's procession and returning holy relics in the main marketplace to the churches so that merchants could set up their carts once again. The activity, the fresh colors, and the warming temperature reminded me of an early spring day in Chicago. Would I ever return to Chicago, to my own life, and to Gerdi?

"My next—and last—apprenticeship will determine the answer to that question," I thought, as I turned into a small lane at the far side of the marketplace. I pondered my impending role as scribe to a *Meistersinger*, poet, playwright, and shoemaker. Surely an artist such as Hans Sachs knows a thing or two about love. But would the simple act of hearing words spoken by Sachs, and then transferring those words to paper, teach me anything? I recalled my months in signal school at Ft. Gordon, during which I had been trained to transcribe the dots and dashes in my headphones to characters on paper without thinking about their meaning. It was all very mechanical, involving no thought on my part. Would this apprenticeship be the same? It was with some misgivings, therefore, that I opened the door under a boot-shaped shingle and quietly entered the shop of Hans Sachs.

My mood changed abruptly when I heard from within the dulcet notes and tender words of "Aura Lee" in a familiar, mellow voice. To announce my presence, I shut the door noisily. The singing changed to an upbeat tempo—something about a teddy bear—to the cadence of a tapping hammer. When the word, "bear," stretched into a crescendo to signal the end of his song, a young man, only a few years my senior, announced, "The King has left the city."

"I know; I was with Him last night," I replied.

"So you were, my young friend," smiled Sachs, "and now you have come to The Lover for instruction on what matters most in life."

"With all due respect, Mr. Sachs, what can a shoemaker, even one who sings like Elvis, teach me about love?"

"Nothing—nothing at all, Bob, and everything."

"Oh, okay, now I understand," I said, smiling to mask my sarcasm.

"It's like this, my *fremder Freund* from the future; I can't teach you how love feels—the exhilaration, the frustration, the ecstasy, the pain—that, only you can learn through experience. But as a Meistersinger, poet, and yes, shoemaker, I can teach you some things *about* love—things other people have experienced."

"No one could know how I feel about Gerdi."

The cobbler turned to His bench, where an upturned boot, a gaping hole worn in its sole, rested on a cobbler's last. He set about repairing the boot, and in the process, initiating my apprenticeship to my Lover. As Hans Sachs set hobnails, his mallet became a baton, tapping iambic feet into the lines of his response to me. The simple verses He recited were of dubious poetic quality, but they communicated clearly the universality of love:

> *My wounded sole—my soul—awakens me to love,*
> *For with the pain of pebbles, comes regard thereof;*
> *And I am but a trav'ler, water on my feet,*
> *In need of human solace to make my life complete.*
>
> *You saw the hole within my soul and made me whole;*
> *You came one day, from far away, to love, console.*
> *The Lover's glue that binds us two as one big shoe*
> *Is reinforced with nails that hurt but bind us too.*
>
> *Without your tender loving, I am just a shell.*
> *Without your sole, your soul, my life would be a hell.*
> *And in the end there is no me there is no you;*
> *There is but one brand new, quite comfortable shoe.*

I stifled a snigger. "You're a good cobbler," I said.

"Okay, so it needs a little polish," laughed Hans, as he trimmed the leather sole with a sharp knife, "but that's how I feel about Kunigunde."

I immediately felt as ease with Hans—not intimidated, as I had been with the Warrior, The Magician, and the King. Hans and I were both young, and we were both in love. I understood that I would need the three less familiar aspects of my Self to carry out my mission, but my Lover was the reason for my being—the meaning of my mission. Love would conquer all.

"Alas, my young apprentice, would that 'twere, would that 'twere."

"I keep forgetting that you guys can read my mind."

"All four of us are inside you, now and forever, Bob. That's why, with the help of Mentor, you can see and hear us. Naturally, we know what is in your every nook and cranny, including your ego."

"Sorry, buddy, I don't mean to joke around, but you seem so much like me," I said.

"That's okay, Bob, I understand. I want you to relate to me, because as your Lover, I am driving you to do what you must to get back to Gerdi and your own life."

"That's for sure, Hans. Each time I went to a new teacher, it was one step closer to home. Mentor helped me to understand that everything I learned from the Warrior, the Magician, and the King would make me a better husband and father. Through it all, I was serving my Lover."

"You have come a long way, Bob, but we have a few things to discuss before you are worthy of your Lover."

"What? I thought that love conquers all…"

"Would that 'twere," repeated the cobbler.

I looked around the cobbler's workshop; the workbench, the simple leather working tools, the shelves of shoes awaiting repair seemed to cry out: "*Dull!*" "*Passionless!*"

"Where I come from, twentieth-century America, it's different, Hans; there are endless possibilities. All you need is love…"

Hans Sachs, the cobbler, rose from his workbench and faced an open window. His voice became that of Hans Sachs the Meistersinger, as he sang into the crisp breeze of early spring:

> *My Kunigunde gives me inspiration,*
> *Our nest of love inspires sweet creation,*
> *Pfennige will fall from angels' wings,*
> *And sweet notes when my Kunigunde sings.*

"Yes, that's right," I exclaimed. "That's how life with Gerdi will be when I get back to my own time, when I get out of the Army, when we are married…"

Hans' sober expression telegraphed his reply: "No, that's not right, Bob. Those are only words to a song. Songs express feelings, but marriage is more than a feeling; marriage is a relationship, and relationships are complicated."

"No! It's simple! Every minute we are together is heaven. Every day is beautiful, even when it's pouring rain, and we miss our *Straßenbahn*. We laugh the time away, we laugh the rain away, we kiss the time away. We are together, and nothing else matters."

"How long have you known each other?"

"All our lives—at least, that's how it seems—months."

"And you have a date whenever the Army lets you out of the *Kaserne*?"

"Sure! I don't get a pass too often, so we make the most of our dates—walks in the park, dinner, special trips…"

"Real life stuff, eh, Bob?"

"Well, it's important to get to know each other, right?"

Hans opened a drawer in His workbench and withdrew a tablet and a piece of charcoal. Handing them to me He said, "Take down my words, Scribe, and mark them well." Pacing the floor of His establishment, Hans declaimed to an audience of well-worn footwear and one love-struck young man:

> *Love is blind, and love is kind, and love can conquer all,*
> *But love, you'll find, must be defined, or it may build a wall.*

"I don't get it, Hans, a wall? Like the Berlin Wall?"

"Higher—more difficult to break down."

"How can that be, Hans? How can the definition of a simple word like 'love' make such a huge difference? I mean, we all know what love means, don't we?"

"Alas, poor Bob! That notion—the notion that *love*, an emotion, a feeling, has one universal connotation—can snare the purest of hearts. Tell me, my friend, how do you feel about Gerdi?"

"She is an angel, everything I have always longed for, she…"

"Do you hear yourself, Bob, Hans interrupted, 'an angel'? Gerdi is *human*, Bob, not an angel. She has good days and bad days, just as you do."

"Yeah, but…"

"And, what was that you said, '…everything I have always longed for'? Who are we talking about here, Gerdi or your own fantasy?"

"Well, when you put it that way, I guess I am sort of blinded by love, but you understand that, don't you Hans? I mean, the way you talked about the woman you love, *Kunigunde*."

"I sure do, Bob, but I understand love in all its dimensions. That's why they call me Lover, and that's why Mentor sent you to me. Your job, if you're going to make Gerdi happy, is to listen to me. Pick up your tablet, Bob." And Hans, the Meistersinger, sang:

Love, true love, is a powerful force,
Tapping the body's innermost source,
Carrying one on a runaway horse,
Galloping on it's own furious course!

A collision of souls on runaway horses
Results in a cancellation of forces
A path emerges from separate courses
With values and mores from different sources.

Can two such souls survive as one
When the volcanic energy's done?
When the fiery lava flow has run
And life together is more than fun?

One may sing, the other refrain,
One may dance, the other disdain.
One may erupt; the other may wane,
One may drive the other insane!

Love's prime organ is the ear
Listen to each other; hear
Cues unspoken, see each tear,
Let her know you're always near.

"I still don't get it, Hans," I said, "All this business about energy and fire sounds good, but I'm not a poet; I'm just a…well, I don't even know what I will be after the Army, and I don't care, as long as Gerdi and I are together. Can you put your advice in more down-to-earth terms?"

Hans sighed. "Okay, Bob," he said, "I'm a cobbler as well as a poet, so I'll give it to you in terms as down to earth as can be—shoes. Follow me."

Hans led me to a workbench at the front of his shop. He picked up a pair of red velvet dance pumps. "These are for fun, Bob, like the good times you have known together with Gerdi."

I nodded. "I attended a ball when I was an apprentice to the King," I said. "I just stood around and sipped wine, but I did see the guests wearing nice shoes like that."

"You have been walking in shoes like these since you met Gerdi. It's no wonder you want your relationship to go on forever. These shoes give you the energy to hurdle all obstacles, to realize your dream of a life together. They are important to your marriage too, Bob, for they represent the joy of living. When times get tough—and they will—remember the good times. Remember these shoes. Put them on—if not for a fancy ball, then at least for a picnic in the park."

I took the velvet pumps from Hans Sachs. I admired their fine craftsmanship. I felt the smooth velvet. I smelled the leather. I thought about what the Lover had said, what the shoes represented. I understood, for the first time, that my relationship with Gerdi must deepen before I could ask her to make a commitment to marriage, to forsake all that she had known to join me in America. She had understood that when I asked for her hand. That's why she had said "nein." It was not that she wasn't ready; it was that she knew *I* wasn't ready.

"Exactly," said Hans.

Would I ever get used to my teachers reading my mind?

Hans took the pumps from me and placed them back on the workbench. He then waved me to a large pair of work boots, one of which was upside down on his cobbler's last, its thick leather sole awaiting

Hans' trimming knife. Hans removed the boot from the last and held it up for my inspection. Its leather upper was scuffed and creased from long wear. It reminded me of my own Army combat boots after a ten-day field maneuver, except that my combat boots were simply caked with mud, rather than actually worn out.

"I have to tell you, Hans, these clodhoppers don't exactly conjure up a romantic image."

"No," replied Hans the Lover, "not to you, but that's because you still have a lot to learn about love."

"Like, maybe, there is more to a lifetime commitment than red velvet pumps?"

"You've got it, little brother," said Hans the cobbler poet. "Take this boot in your hands, Bob; look at the heel, worn from miles of walking to the fields in the morning and back home at night—home to a *Frau* and *Kinder* who depend on those fields for life. The heel wore slowly but consistently, the way the barley and wheat in those fields grew, the way the bonds of love in that home grew.

"Feel the creases in the rough leather, Bob. The man who wears these boots must squat to know the earth intimately, for the earth nurtures his loved ones. He must hold the earth in his hands to feel its texture, moisture, and to observe any day-to-day changes.

"Smell the boot, Bob. Does it smell sweet, like a freshly cut rose? Does it smell intoxicating, like Gerdi's perfume the night you proposed to her? No? How does it smell then—like cow dung from the fields—cow dung that feeds the fields that grow the crops for the man's family? Like sweat—sweat yielded willingly in a labor of love, year after year? Like dirt—dirt that nourishes and sustains life and that allows roots to grow?"

I felt the weight of the boot in my hands. I thought of love as portrayed in the movies, all romance and excitement. I thought of Gerdi, so familiar with hardship, orphaned at birth, playing in the rubble of post-war Nürnberg, surviving disease, malnutrition, and the almost super human effort required to rebuild her city and her life under American occupation and the Communist threat from the east. She was wise beyond her years; she had seen through the star-crossed, shallow feelings of a callow young man. She had said "nein." But she was patient; she recognized a good boy who could become a good man. "This is a good boot," I said.

Hans sensed that I was a bit too eager to take up the millstone for the wrong reason—as a token of my love, rather than as the necessary means to fulfillment of my own Lover. Taking the work boot from my hand, he recited:

> *This humble boot may be your fate*
> *Should you follow your Lover's instruction.*
> *Its path may lead you to your mate*
> *Or to ultimate ego destruction.*
> *A martyr can humiliate*
> *In attempting to manage seduction,*
> *So sacrifice, but communicate*
> *Your Warrior, King, and Magician!*

I listened to the Lover's words, attempting to make sense of them. "So were you serious about all that hard work, Hans? It sounds like you're changing your tune."

"Not at all, Bob," the Lover replied. "Indeed, you must don the boots of a worker; wear them not as a mask of tragedy, but joyfully, for they carry you home. They feed your loved ones and keep them warm."

Placing the work boot next to its mate on the last, the cobbler moved on. "Here is quality," he said, admiring the soft leather and fine detail of a *Bürger's* shoe. "According to the sumptuary laws of Nürnberg, such a shoe may be worn only by citizens of stature."

My mind raced ahead; would I ever be a "citizen of stature?" Would I have an office on the 26th floor of a skyscraper in downtown Chicago, overlooking Lake Michigan? Would people respect my wealth and power? Would they have to make appointments with my secretary to see me? Would they call me "sir" and give me a little extra space as I walk the corridors?

How different that would be from my upbringing on the South Side—shunned by other kids because of my harelip and ignored by teachers because of my speech defect! How different that would be from having to eke out a living as a door-to-door salesman, begging for people's attention, only to have doors slammed in my face hundreds of times a day! How different that would be from this life as a lowly G.I., my every minute controlled by superiors who told me what to do, what to wear, when to eat, when to sleep, and how I should present myself—"military deportment"! How I longed to be a citizen of stature!

"You're losing it, little brother," said Hans, reading my thoughts.

"I would do anything to wear shoes like that, to be a citizen of stature," I replied honestly.

"As your inner Lover, may I ask why?"

"Well, to provide for my family, of course," I replied.

"I see," said Hans the Lover. "Would you work hard?"

"Yes!"

"Would you be very clever?"

"Yes!"

"Would you put in long hours?"

"Yes!"

"Would you be willing to relocate your family?"

"Yes!"

"Would you be willing to travel, to be away from your family for a week at a time?"

"Yes!"

"Would you give your allegiance to your company?"

"Yes!"

"Would you say and do anything to advance your career?"

"Yes," I blurted, in all honestly.

"Then I can't help you. Get out of my shop!" Hans the Lover—My inner Lover—faced me squarely with his cobbler's hammer in one hand and his trim knife in the other. He was deadly serious.

So you see, Alex, if taken for granted, Love can be a tough cookie!

CHAPTER THIRTEEN

The Dark Side

I left the shop. A cold wind whipped the folds of my monk's robe as I made my way down the cobblestone street to the marketplace. I was upset by my abrupt dismissal from the Lover's workshop. I was also hungry, I realized, for it was mid-day. My breakfast, a hard roll and cup of tea, had not prepared me for the energy-sapping drama of Hans Sachs. "Hans and I were getting along so well," I thought, "until he showed me those damned fancy shoes. Why shouldn't I want to make something of myself? He tricked me with all those stupid questions. Is he trying to say that Gerdi would rather be married to some poor schnook than to a hotshot businessman?"

Wealthy merchants and city officials—citizens of stature—were streaming into an imposing *Gasthaus* facing the market square. I felt the little bag of coins Monk had given me and thought, "W*hy not*? I'll hobnob with citizens of stature and get a taste of the good life—literally."

Inside, serving girls fussed over the *Bürgers*, who seemed quite pleased with themselves. I realized that I was a bit out of place, so I took a spot at a table in a dark corner of the restaurant. No one paid attention to the "monk," so I waited patiently while the *citizens of stature* were served. I observed their shoes. "Very nice," I thought, "I'll have a pair of those shoes one day." Soon all the other tables were full, and three merchants sat at my table with only a nod at the "monk." I was accustomed to the silent treatment; it was, after all, my purpose in adopting that role. I had worked out a system of gestures for simple transactions. When the serving girl came to my table, she greeted the businessmen and took their orders. When their food came, I simply pointed to one of their plates and then to a glass of wine. The serving girl hesitated. Monks seldom entered this elegant establishment, but she would serve me if I did not expect a free ride. Catching her meaning, I placed some coins on the table. She nodded and turned away.

My semi-invisible status permitted the men at my table to speak freely. They spoke of dealings with spice traders from the Levant and silk merchants from Italy. They bragged about financial coups with Augsburg bankers. They berated Nürnberg artisans who demanded outrageous sums for their silver and pewter and ridiculed customers in Frankfurt who paid many times that price for resale. "These men are successful," I thought, "just look at the way they are dressed—puffy pantaloons, ruffled collars, and feathered hats—not my style, but unmistakably rich."

Satisfied with my *Mittagessen* and warmed by two tankards of red wine, I left the Gasthaus and crossed the Pegnitz River. "To hell with the shoe guy," I thought, as I wandered aimlessly through a maze of tiny streets and alleys in an unfamiliar section of the old city. "The men in that *Gasthaus* are clever, wealthy, and respected. They must be the happiest people on earth."

I halted, for the road ahead was blocked by pigs being driven to the river for a bath. "Look at that poor guy," I thought, "in his rough shirt and old hat, his boots splattered by pig shit. I'll bet he never gets the stink out of his clothes. He'll sell his pigs to one of those clever merchants, who will turn them over to a sausage maker for ten times what he paid this fellow."

The swine had cleared the road, leaving only a strong reminder of their presence. I pinched my nostrils shut and walked on. I came to the city wall and turned to walk the narrow street that ran along the inside of the wall. Safely disguised as a monk, I felt much better than I had when I left Hans' shoe repair shop. "What a loser, I thought, trying to make me ashamed for wanting to make it big. No wonder he's just a cobbler—and a lousy poet. I'm going to be rich some day, no matter what, and then Gerdi will agree to marry me!"

The sound of a woman's voice interrupted my reverie: "Hey you, monk, are ya lost? Or maybe ya came to get something warm and sweet. Whatcha got under that robe?"

Startled, I realized that I had wandered into the red light district of Nürnberg, a strip of buildings facing the inside of the city wall, where women brazenly display themselves in the windows and call out to men who congregate there. I blushed under the cowl of my robe but ignored the woman. "How sad," I thought, "women reduced to prostitution, having sex with any strange man willing to pay—any pathetic weirdo who doesn't have the balls to court a woman." I thought of Gerdi: "How could anyone take pleasure in the favors of a whore when real love is waiting at home?"

It was then that I noticed the man speaking with a buxom young lady hanging out of a window at his eye level. The man wore a feathered hat, ruffled collar, puffy pantaloons, and elegant shoes of the type I had seen in the cobbler's shop. He was one of the men who had shared my table in the Gasthaus! He was...*a citizen of stature.*

The interaction between this citizen of stature—rich, successful, respected in the community—and the prostitute, a woman of the lowest caste, was fascinating to watch. She was clearly in charge, a master of sexual manipulation, alternately massaging the man's ego and mocking his submissiveness. His furtive glances at passersby betrayed his fear of being exposed. "What weakness, I thought, would cause a man of high standing and obvious accomplishment to risk it all for a cheap thrill?"

The man leaned forward and said something that made the woman recoil. She shrieked at him and withdrew from the window. The man walked quickly away. He looked back at the whorehouse once or twice, as though he feared someone might follow him. His only shadow—hardly noticeable, and certainly not a threat—was a humble figure in the vestments of a monk. The man turned a corner and entered a small pub.

Curious, I followed the man into the dim, noisy pub. The *Bürger* was clearly out of his element among the other patrons—rough laborers consuming sausages, black bread, and beer. The man seated himself at a small table away from the crowd. I sat in a dark, back corner where I could discreetly observe the man. A serving wench brought him a bottle of red wine. "He has been here before," I thought. I placed a coin on the table and gestured to the girl that I would like a small glass of wine.

The *Bürger* drank fast, filling his glass three times before leaning back in his chair. He caught me watching him under my cowl and demanded, "What are you looking at?"

"Uh oh," I thought, "a confrontation. I don't think this guy is on Mentor's approved list of masculine archetypes. Have I assimilated enough sixteenth-century German to communicate with him?"

I did my best to portray an Irish monk, so that my limited German would not be too suspicious. "Who knows," I thought, "maybe the merchant has picked up some English in his travels."

"Begging your pardon brother," I intoned, "ye seemed distraught. If ye tattle me superior no tale of a monk's broken vow, I shall lend an ear to ye and hold it all silent within."

The man's face broke with relief. Here, at last, was a confidant to whom he could pour out his dark secrets like wine. "*Vater*," he began, "what manner of man do you see before you?"

I replied, "I see a man wrapped in the garments of wealth and success, a citizen of stature, respected by all."

"*Ja*," said the merchant, his face sagging, "deese clothes are made von der finest stuff—even von Ireland, where maybe you come von, *Vater*."

"Yes," I said.

"I have been to your homeland, *Vater*. I have been to many lands to make trade. I come back always to Nürnberg mit beautiful stuff to sell in da market. Und da people buy it always. I go again und again to buy und to sell. I am rich man—fine clothes, beek house. I marry woman von good family. More money."

"Are you happy my brother?"

"No, *Vater*. I must look happy, wear happy clothes, wear happy face... but I am lonely, sad man."

"In spite of your wealth and respect in the city?"

"I tink maybe because of it."

"Because of it?" I could not believe what I was hearing.

"*Ja*, you see, I vas not born into dis life. I come von der land. Mein *Vater* var a poor farmer. These hands vorked the soil until I left my village at fourteen."

"So young!"

"*Ja*, vell, I was big enough to do man's work. I joined a caravan of merchants. I take care of oxen and mules; I take care of wagons."

"And you learned the trade..."

"*Ja*, I go von town to town, buy here, sell der. I go to other lands even. I learn to speak many tongues, to talk like big traders. I learn vhy people buy things, how to make money."

"And you finally came to Nürnberg."

"I go in Nürnberg many times. Roads von east, sout, vest, nort go trou' Nürnberg. Every time I go trou' Nürnberg, I get more money. I get rich. I meet beek people. I marry daughter of beek man, und I become beek man."

"But not a happy man," I said.

"*Nein*," said the man, I marry for money, und I get more money, but not happiness."

"Not…love?"

"Not luf," answered the man, "I vant luf, so I give her tings. I must work hard to make money for dese tings. I feel like slave."

"How does she feel?" I asked.

"I don't know."

"You don't know? How can you not know? She is your wife!"

"I don't know. I go on caravan to buy merchandise, to make money. I come home, give her tings, but she is not happy. I don't know."

"So you go to girls behind the wall."

The man's face registered panic. "You know?"

"I know, *Mein Herr*, but I shan't tell a soul."

The man looked as though he might cry. "I look like beek, fancy man in marketplace, but I am lonely, sick in mein soul, Vater."

Remembering the words of Hans Sachs, the cobbler-poet, I intoned the Lover's words:

> *Love is blind, and love is kind, and love can conquer all,*
> *But love, you'll find, must be defined, or it may build a wall*

I thought it ironic that I, an alien, an American kid, should be giving marital advice to a great merchant, a man whose shoes I wanted to wear. "It must be the monk's vestments," I thought. "*Mein Herr*," I said, "you must go home and talk to your wife. Ask her what is important to her. You may find that giving her *things* is not so important as giving her *yourself*. Tell her how you feel, and what you need. Ask her how she feels and what she needs. Listen to her. Listen with your heart as well as your ears."

"Thank you, *Vater*," the man said. He left the rest of his bottle and walked out of the pub, his head held a bit higher, a look of resolve in his eyes. The other men in the pub glanced at the *Bürger* and at the "monk" before redirecting their attention to their sausage and beer.

I left the pub as well, walking slowly in the direction of the main market, my thoughts tumbling into consciousness in pace with my steps.

"That man...that 'citizen of stature'... his fine clothes, the respect shown to him in the marketplace and the *Gasthaus*...he was my idol, the symbol of success for me. I told the Lover—my own inner lover— that I would be willing to sacrifice time with my loved ones, that I would do anything, say anything for some soulless corporation, just to wear the shoes of a *citizen of stature*. Why? For the love of the corporation? No, that corporation would not love me; it would toss me out like an old pair of shoes if my removal would improve the bottom line. No, it would be all about me—my self-esteem, my ego. I could be important— no longer the little boy who 'talks funny,' who is 'dumb,' who is 'ugly.' Maybe someone would love me.

"Now someone does love me, despite my imperfections, despite my immaturity. She must see something in me. How can I be worthy of that love?"

My reverie was interrupted when I came to the Pegnitz River and became aware of my surroundings. Before me stood the cottage of the hangman—my first teacher, the Warrior. "What had I learned from the Warrior," I mused. "'A man's gotta do what a man's gotta do.' That's it— duty—duty to God, to country, to the role in which he is cast. The executioner did not want to torture and kill his victims. Hell, one of them was his own brother. But he did, because it was his duty; if he did the unthinkable, another man would be spared the task. Soldiers do that. Medics do that; they tap into their Warrior to aid injured men on the battlefield, even when the victims violently resist help." I was struck by an insight: A man who loves a woman must sometimes confront her—deal with important issues instead of avoiding conflict, as I tend to do. Was my inability to manage conflict one of the red flags that Gerdi had seen?

I walked east along the south bank of the Pegnitz, toward the marketplace. I paused on the *Museumbrücke* to check the progress of work on the Holy Ghost Hospital. Hans Behaim was a highly skilled architect with years of specialized training—a true Magician. From Hans Behaim, I had learned that a real man must become apprentice to his own Magician—that inner drive to learn, to acquire specialized skills, and to continue to learn throughout his lifetime. Knowledge is its own reward, I knew, but more importantly to me at this time, was the financial security it promised to Gerdi. When I asked for her hand in marriage, I had given no forethought to practical matters, such as making a living. Would we not live on love? Gerdi, a bit older and wiser than I, had considered my lack of education and experience. She remembered years of deprivation following World War II and understood the strain it could put on a relationship. She loved me very much—so much that she wanted our marriage to have every chance to succeed. Was that why, when her adoring, sincere, naïve suitor popped the question, she had said *"nein"*?

As I crossed from the bridge into the open market, I recalled the procession of Charles V. Throngs of loyal subjects—and one lone, would-be assassin—greeted their emperor. "My inadvertent thwarting of the assassination had led to my brief internship with Charles V, Holy Roman Emperor," I thought. "Why had Monk arranged that? Had Charles V portrayed my inner King, my ability and willingness to be a leader? How would leadership contribute to my role as Gerdi's husband?"

I pondered the meaning of leadership. "Is leadership simply being the biggest, baddest warrior, forcing others to submit to your authority? No… a warrior does what he has to do. That takes courage, and courage is part of leadership, but it's not enough. What about magical energy? Surely, a leader has the ability to gather facts, to analyze them, and come up with the best solutions to problems. That's what university professors and think tank analysts do. But who listens to them? Well, leaders listen to those guys," I thought, "and people listen to leaders!" I thought of Charles V presiding over the Diet. Representatives from every patch of the crazy quilt that made up the Holy Roman Empire had attended, each with his own agenda. Charles V, the King, had shown the courage to stand before them and the intelligence to understand their strengths and their needs. He could have published a scholarly paper in *The Psychological Journal of the Holy Roman Empire,* Vol. 557, Summer, 1522. But he is an emperor—a King. He *listened* to princes and dukes from far-flung corners of the empire. He weighed their interests against the greater good and achieved a consensus among them. This he could not have accomplished through raw power alone. He went to the people and *loved* them!

"A man must be a king within his own home," I realized. "He must love his queen and all in their little kingdom enough to listen to them, to draw upon his own Warrior and Magician and those of his loved ones to lead them to consensus—a path all happily follow—together."

Under the cowl of my robe, I had been lost in the world of my own thoughts, but my feet seemed to know where I should go. Jolted by a familiar voice into awareness of my surroundings, my eyes rested on Monk holding open a door under a large silhouette of a shoe—the sign of Hans Sachs the cobbler/poet—my inner Lover.

CHAPTER FOURTEEN

Finding My Father

Alex, this is when I learned that you can't understand a person—especially a person close to you—until you stop thinking about how that person treated you and start thinking about how life has treated that person. To understand is to forgive is to love.

With a slight bow to Mentor, I entered the Lover's workshop. I could hear Hans hammering soles and doing his Elvis imitation:

> *Ready! Teddy!*
> *Go, man go!*
> *I got a gal that I love so...*

"I get it, Hans," I called. "Yes, I'm *ready* to listen."

Hans rose to his feet above the barrier of shoes piled on his workbench, a wide grin spreading across his face. "Oh, there you are, Bob, did you have a nice walk?"

"Somehow, I think you know all about it, Hans."

"Yes," we enjoyed the show, Bob." It was Mentor speaking.

"So you do get out of your hole in the wall," I said. "What is the occasion?"

"The show."

"The show?"

"You're gonna love this, little brother," said Hans. "Step into my lounge."

"Your *lounge?*" I laughed, "Why does a cobbler need a lounge?"

Hans lifted his chin in mock pomposity. "I'll have you know, young man, that I am renowned as a poet and *Meistersinger*. Shoe repair is just my day job. A poet needs a study—a den of solitude to reflect and commune with his muse."

"Okay, whatever," I said, as I followed Hans. Mentor brought up the rear.

A sign on the door to the lounge stated, "Man Cave." I entered, half expecting to see Neanderthals clad in animal skins, huddled around a campfire, chewing on huge thighbones. Instead, I saw what looked like a paneled rec room in a Chicago bungalow. The dark floor tiles and dropped ceiling reminded me of my boyhood friend's basement back on Ridgeland Avenue. The only natural light filtered through glass block windows, but fluorescent fixtures in the ceiling and an Old Style beer lamp hanging over the pool table provided all the light I needed to see the occupants of the stools at the bar along the wall: Franz Schmidt, the Nuremberg hangman, Hans Behaim, the architect, and Emperor Charles V!

"I believe you know my friends," said Hans, the Lover.

I was astounded. "But don't you gentlemen have places to go and things to do? I mean, there must be someone waiting to be tortured, a new cathedral to be designed, a kingdom at the edge of your empire to be defended...."

"You are stuck in real-time thinking," said Mentor, "but we will not hold that against you. Suffice it to say that the Warrior, the Magician, the King, and the Lover are with you—within you—all the time. These men are archetypes of those qualities—those energies—that are a part of you. You need only to summon them when they are required to fulfill your mature, masculine mission."

I was confused and feeling dizzy. "But how...how did I get here, and why? And where is 'here?' For that matter, when is 'now?'"

"Take a deep breath," said Mentor. "Look at me. Put everything else out of your mind. Take another deep breath...now another...and another. Focus on me. Breathe.... What do you see?"

In this strange place, surrounded by these men, these manifestations of the composite man that I must become if I hoped to be worthy of Gerdi, I understood that I was facing a rite of initiation, a test. My answer to Monk's question must be acceptable.

"I see a wise man, Mentor, I see a guide who can lead me to sources of courage, of intellectual growth and leadership. I see a guide who can lead me to love. I see a guide who can teach me to draw from within myself the courage to fight for right, the curiosity to uncover the mysteries of life, the will to lead others to realize their own potential for the collective good. I see a guide who can teach me to access my Lover energy—the courage to confront differences with love, the motivation to harness technology for the care of my loved ones, the humility to lead through service for the benefit of those who would follow. I see a guide who can lead me to my Lover energy—God energy—that infuses the universe, displacing fear and hatred, displacing negative thoughts with positive thoughts, displacing greed with generosity, replacing sordid urges with purity. I see the God within."

"Lo, I am with you always, even unto the end of the world, saith the Lord," said Mentor. "We *are* talking God here, Bob. God is inside you. Just listen; knock, and your soul will be opened unto you. It's all there—everything you will need."

Struck dumb by the revelation that my entire ordeal—emerging from a tunnel connecting the SS Kaserne to the sixteenth-century city of Nuremberg; being rescued by a monk who became known to me as Mentor; and being apprenticed to the hangman, architect, emperor and poet—was all an altered state of consciousness, an experience of the Collective Unconscious, as Mentor would say, I could only murmur, "How do I snap out of this? How do I get back to my life—to Gerdi?"

Mentor pointed to a barstool. "Have a seat, Bob, and let us review before your final exam."

"My final exam?"

"Surely, you don't think that all this training was meaningless, Bob. You came here to learn what you must know to carry out your role as a mature man—the man Gerdi needs and deserves. Your final exam will be life itself, and it will commence within the hour."

I took my seat, flanked by Mentor and Hans the Lover. It was then that I noticed mounted to the wall behind the bar, what looked like a television, but much bigger and slimmer. I was puzzled: "Where is the cathode ray tube?" I thought. Then Mentor picked up a plastic thing, about the size of a pack of cigarettes, covered with little buttons. He pointed it at the television, and the screen lit up immediately—in full color!

"What is that thing?" I asked.

"Haven't you ever seen a TV?" asked the Magician.

"Not like that," I replied, "How did you get it to show colors?"

"Oh, I forgot," said Mentor, "you came here when televisions were still pretty primitive—black and white, tiny pictures, three channels, and no remote. How did you cope with it?"

"Hey, wait a minute! How can you have television in the sixteenth century? Wait! How can you even have electricity? Aggh!" My chest heaved, and my head was spinning.

Mentor placed his hand on my shoulder. "Relax, Bob, and have a beer." He drew *seven* mugs of good German beer from a large keg. We settled in to watch the screen.

Mentor asked, "What do you see, Bob?"

An image of my father, who had died five years earlier, appeared. He was lying on the battered couch in the "front room" of our old house on Ridgeland Avenue. "That couch was where my teenaged sister slept," I said. "Between the couch and the front door was what we called a 'bookcase'; it was a dark walnut cabinet, about thirty inches wide and four feet high. A piece of faded cloth covered the open front. The cabinet contained a stack of comic books: Superman, Bugs Bunny, and Donald Duck I loved the adventures of Huey, Dewey, and Louie as 'Junior Woodchucks.' A pencil sharpener was screwed to the top of that cabinet, and my plastic model of a fighter jet sat next to it. My dad would place his beer or wine glass there when he paced back and forth, watching the fights or 'The Honeymooners' on our twelve-inch black and white TV. On the other side of the front door, in front of the picture window, was a big, wooden rocking chair where my older brother watched White Sox games, often sucking on a lemon. He and I shared a sofa bed in the same 'front room,' next to an oil stove, the only source of heat in that four-room house.

"One of my daily chores had been to haul a five-gallon can of fuel oil from one of the fifty-five gallon drums in the garage out back to the stove. Filling the can, I pretended to be milking a cow, as I had once seen my uncle do on his Iowa farm. After that visit, when I was nine years old, I decided that I wanted to be a farmer when I grew up. Unfortunately, the can had a tendency to slosh 'milk'—well, oil—as I carried it through the enclosed back porch, kitchen, and dining room to the stove in the 'front room,' giving the run-down shack that we called home a characteristic odor. My parents' room hardly qualified as a bedroom, with no door and only a curtain across one wall to serve as the sole closet for a family of six—five after my oldest sister married."

My first feeling, upon seeing the image of my father loafing on the couch was that he should have been doing something to improve the house. The sagging floors, rotten siding—everything about that old shack was substandard. It was a slum, the oldest house in the neighborhood. All the other houses on the block were well-maintained brick bungalows or frame homes. Why had he not picked up a hammer and attempted to fix up the place? Why had my father done nothing to improve our family's living conditions? Why had he not worked a second job or given up smoking and drinking to scrape up the money for a better home? Seeing my dad on the screen like that, loafing on the couch, I felt old, familiar feelings: disgust, alienation, contempt, and even hatred for that house, for my father, and for myself, for he, my father, and that house were all mixed up inside me.

"Growing up in that house affected how you felt about yourself, didn't it Bobby?"

I took my eyes off the screen to see who was speaking. It was my own father, seated at the far end of the bar!

As I looked at the screen and at my dad, looking as alive as the other five men in Hans Sachs' lounge, I became aware of the thoughts, memories, and feelings in my father's mind. I saw my father as a coddled child in an affluent household, sheltered from physical exertion because of rheumatic fever. I saw my father as a young man, making his way in the big city, meeting his future wife, and falling in love. I saw an earnest young dad, swinging his little girl in Jackson Park during the Great Depression. I saw my father traveling to New York City in search of employment, only to learn that the job he had been told about was no longer available. I saw my father hitchhiking back to Chicago, humiliated, as his wife supported their little family on her tips as a waitress. I saw my father back at work in factories geared up for wartime production. I saw my father moving his growing family from one South Side apartment to another, seeking more space at a time when no houses were being built. I saw my father jump at the opportunity to buy a little house on Ridgeland Avenue, just as his wife announced that she was expecting their fourth child. It was small and run-down, but it was a house!

I saw my father, unskilled at things involving tools, overwhelmed at the prospect of maintaining and expanding a handyman special. As the thrill of home ownership wore off, and the post-war building boom filled magazines with photos of dream homes, his discontented wife berated him for his ineptitude. He was not a handyman, and as a factory worker, he could not afford to hire contractors. He was not a war veteran, so there was no G.I. Bill to help him buy into the tracts springing up in the suburbs. His indulgent parents, lack of knowledge and skill, and his Depression-beaten spirit had left him unprepared to relate to his wife's concerns in an assertive, loving way. Her discontent turned to resentment, then to hostility. He reacted by withdrawing from his wife and from his children, going for long walks or escaping in TV when he was not at work.

I understood all this, and so much more, in a flash of insight when my father appeared in Hans Sachs' "man cave."

CHAPTER FIFTEEN

A Vision of Heaven

"What's going on?" I asked. "Who is that guy who looks so much like my dad, and how did I suddenly understand all this new stuff about my father after I viewed the image of him on that fancy television?"

Mentor, Charles V, Hans Sachs, and the Hangman turned to the Magician, Hans Behaim, who responded, "Okay, I shall take this query." Behaim, as the archetype of magical energy, the energy that I would later draw upon to learn and apply electronics wizardry and to master all manner of arcane knowledge needed to survive in a technological jungle, assumed the didactic manner of a college professor delivering his first lecture of the semester.

"Welcome to Metaphysics 911, Introduction to the Principles of Proportional Pleasure and Pain. This is an advanced course in the 4-P theory of afterlife based on scientific principles, a rigorous scrutiny of literature, and empirical evidence."

"The afterlife," I thought, "...am I dead?" I raised my hand.

"No," said the Magician.

"Oh jeez," I thought, "of course, he's reading my mind. I keep forgetting these guys can do that. I'd better hold my questions."

"On the contrary, young man," responded the Magician, "one of the objectives of this course is to stimulate questions. Critical thinking is encouraged."

I just nodded. I focused on my breathing, trying to clear my mind of the whirlwind of thoughts in my head.

"Now," continued the Magician, "let us begin with the following axioms, synthesized from a review of great literature, pan-theological notions of God, and commonly accepted principles of justice.

"*Axiom I: God is just.* '...the gods are just,' said Shakespeare, and in *Paradise Lost,* Milton said that the ways of God are just. Do you accept that axiom, Bob?"

"I wonder, sometimes, when a young person dies of cancer, or when I see the rich get richer on the sweat of their workers. Yet, I must believe that 'what goes around comes around,' as they say. Heaven and Hell must be God's way to even the score. So, yeah, I accept the axiom that God is just."

"*Axiom II: God is omniscient.* 'He telleth the number of the stars; he calleth them all by their names. Great is our Lord, and of great power: his understanding is infinite.'"

"That's from the Bible," I said, "Psalms, I believe."

"Correct."

"Okay," I said, "I do accept the axiom that God knows everything."

"*Axiom III: Heaven is being with God.* What do you think of that?"

"Well, all those years attending that little Baptist church on the South Side, the Sunday School teachers and ministers talked about being 'saved,' and I assumed that being 'saved' meant going to heaven after I die. But they didn't go into details. Now that you mention it, though, I remember Jesus saying something like: 'I go to prepare a place for you... I will come again and receive you unto myself; that where I am, there you may be also.' So, okay, you're right, I guess; if you consider Jesus as being one with God, then in heaven you would be with Jesus, hence with God."

"So heaven is being with God."

"Yeah."

"Just testing your understanding."

"Yes sir."

"*Axiom IV: Heaven is being one with God.*"

"Well yeah…"

"Hold it right there, young man! What kind of response is, 'Well yeah'? Where's your critical thinking? Did I offer any proof that 'heaven is being one with God'? I want you to push back!"

I cleared my throat. "Actually, sir, Axiom III, which we discussed at some length, established that heaven is being *with* God. But how can we make the leap from being *with* God to being *one with* God? I think of it this way: Anyone who has ever seen a rotting corpse knows that the physical body returns to its chemical constituents after death. However, something remains—something intangible, yet real—something powerful enough to cause the chest to heave, the throat to throb, the eyes to tear in real people who survive the deceased. That something is love."

"Hear! Hear!" interjected Hans Sachs, the Lover.

"And how does this death-defying power you describe...love...relate to a oneness with God?" asked Hans Behaim, the Magician.

"Love is the fundamental essence," I replied, "and God *is* love. If you need a reference, check The First Epistle of St. John, Chapter 4, verse 8. There is no difference between our fundamental essence and that of God. Thus, when we leave our physical body, we become one with God."

"Excellent! Your logic is impeccable, and your conviction is powerful."

"I think of it as faith, sir."

"Yes, well, let us conclude. *Axiom V: Heaven is eternal.*"

"Definitely! Remember that Bible verse...'the gift of God is eternal life'?"

"Right—so we are in agreement about these five axioms: God is just; God is omniscient; heaven is being with God; heaven is being one with God; and heaven is eternal."

"Yep."

"Let us flesh this out," said the Magician. "If in heaven we become one with God, who is omniscient, we will then be omniscient."

"Makes sense," I agreed. "We'll know everything. That sounds pretty cool."

"We are in agreement that God is just."

"Yes sir. That was Axiom I."

"Hence the name of this theory: '*Proportional* Pleasure and Pain.'"

"Proportional?"

"Correct. The heaven/hell dichotomy, in which souls are sorted into two classifications: saved and damned, is a bit like a teeter-totter; the candidate for salvation is weighed against his or her lifetime behaviors. Certain individuals are easy to classify. For example, Adolph Hitler would clearly be cast into the flames of hell..."

"You got that right!" I interjected.

The Magician lowed his chin, looking over his glasses at me.

"As I was saying," he continued. "On the other hand, a beneficent figure such as Mother Teresa would clearly be worthy of heavenly bliss."

"Clearly," I thought, but I held my tongue.

Mentor produced a slate board and chalk. "Thank you," said the Magician, who then drew a Bell Curve. "Let us consider human behavior in terms of 'sins' and 'good works,'" he said. "The example to which we previously referred, i.e., Hitler and Mother Teresa, occupy the lowest positions on opposite sides of this bell-shaped slope. Most individuals, according to the Bell theory, fall somewhere between these extremes, with the greatest concentration on either side of the peak."

"Neither perfect nor terrible," I offered.

"Yes, if you prefer to put it in simple terms."

I considered the drawing and the fact that, according to Magician's explanation, most people are neither completely holy nor terribly wicked. "So for a guy at the peak—the mid-point between really good and really bad, a few little sins could put him over the top—into hell!"

"Precisely. Does that strike you as fair—just?"

"No, it's just like you said—a teeter totter. It's not balanced, not fair."

"Contrary to Axiom I: God is just."

"Yeah…I see what you're saying," I said. "So what does your theory have to say about that?"

"That will become clear when we summarize the principles of Proportional Pleasure and Pain with the following exposition:

Upon 'graduation' from human existence, all individuals enter the afterlife, which we may designate 'heaven'—an eternal life in which these subjects become one with the omniscient God, thus gaining an all-encompassing knowledge. The secrets of the universe: science, history, psychology, philosophy—everything—are revealed to them. This knowledge is 100% accurate, deeply profound, and instantly available."

"Wow! That does sound like heaven! Imagine the ability to know everything! But wait a minute; where does the 'God is just' part come in? How is it fair that everyone goes to heaven and gets to know everything?"

"Excellent question, young man. Has it ever occurred to you that knowledge may be a blessing or a curse?"

"Hmmm…I guess there are things I don't want to know, like what my mom and dad did behind closed doors…"

"How about the knowledge that everyone who has ever lived is watching every moment of your life, including things *you* have done behind closed doors?"

"Wait a minute! That's part of it?"

"That is part of it."

"That would be kind of painful."

"Hence the name…"

"Pleasure and *Pain*," I broke in.

"Exactly," said the Magician, "Heaven, the eternal existence, will entail a complete review of the lives of everyone who has ever lived—*by* everyone who has ever lived."

I was baffled. "Are you saying that there's going to be some kind of huge auditorium, and we're going to spend eternity viewing movies of everyone who has ever lived? How is that even possible?"

The Magician patiently answered, "The technology is far beyond that of your mid-twentieth century or of that which will be developed in your lifetime. It is, in fact, far beyond human comprehension. You must accept, as an article of faith, that eternity will be a revelation of all knowledge, accessed as required to understand and judge the actions of every human who has ever lived, including yourself."

"Okay, let me get this straight. The whole world will be watching every move I have ever made…"

"Right…"

"And everyone will know not only what I did, but *why*, 'cause they will have access to my history, the facts behind the circumstances, and the psychological knowledge to understand my behavior."

"Excellent!" exclaimed the Magician. "So, to the extent that any of your actions reviewed by this universal body of judges, who know all the extenuating circumstances, are virtuous, you will feel the pleasure of approbation."

"That's the pleasure part of the equation."

"Yes, and your pleasure or pain will be proportional to the pride or shame you feel as a result of full disclosure to this supremely qualified body of judges."

"Which includes those closest to you in life? Yikes!"

"Exactly."

"No more teeter totter: good…bad…good…bad…bad…oops! Off to

Hell with you! Do not cross GO."

"Exactly."

"Well, it's fair, I guess—'just,' as you say."

"Axiom I," verified the Magician.

"So, does this account for the sudden insights I had when Dad's image came up on that screen? Is this the afterlife?"

The Magician smiled. "Hardly, Bob. This was only a preview—a rough prototype. You don't get the full version until you die."

"The *full version*?"

"Yes. In your unfortunate mortal condition, your perception is limited by your senses of sight, hearing, touch, smell, and taste. The primitive insights you experienced are mere thoughts, processed by your physical brain." When you are released from mortal bounds, you will have unlimited, instant access to all the information that has ever been generated: every molecular transformation, the length of every hair that has landed on every barber's floor, the orbit of every heavenly body, every action and thought of every human, baboon, and dolphin that has ever lived."

"Isn't it going to be awfully boring, spending eternity reviewing the lives of people, if I already know everything?"

"Admittedly, it would be boring, *if* you already knew everything. Note, however, that I said you will have unlimited, instant *access* to all the information that has ever been generated. As you review each person's life, and as others view yours, the information required to fully understand the circumstances, options, and motivations governing that person's behavior will automatically present itself."

"Like driving a car with automatic transmission," I said. "It knows when to shift gears and does it automatically, so the driver can concentrate on the road."

"Good analogy," said the Magician. "Judges will be able to focus on the purity of the subject's intentions—or the evil underlying them. Subjects of this life review—this depth analysis—will truly bare their souls to scrutiny by God for we will all be with God, one with God."

"This is an interesting theory of the afterlife," I said. "It's unlike anything I learned in Sunday school, but then, we didn't really get into a concrete description of heaven. Everyone wanted to go there, but no one knew why."

"Now you have a better idea."

"Yeah, the afterlife will be heaven and hell. How much of each depends on how we live our lives here on earth."

So, Alex, this is my vision of Heaven—the time and knowledge to completely understand the "what" and "why" of life. I can't say that I'm looking forward to sharing my innermost secrets with everyone, but I guess it's fair. What about you? What kind of heaven do you envision?

Chapter Sixteen

Final Exams

"You have analyzed the abstruse principles of Proportional Pleasure and Pain and synthesized them into one succinct, accurate, statement, Bob. I am satisfied that you have the perspicacity and perseverance required to decipher the most arcane mysteries within the pantology. I therefore support your graduation."

Mentor nodded, and then he looked at Warrior, King, and Lover. "Graduation requires unanimous consent. Each of you has had an opportunity to evaluate Bob's progress. What say you?"

The Nuremberg hangman, the Warrior archetype, handed his ax to me. "Are you willing to do your duty, to fight for what is right?"

I thought of my natural tendency to avoid conflict and how it seemed to frustrate Gerdi's need for honest, open communication. I remembered the hangman's courage when called upon to do his duty, even to carry out a sentence imposed on his own brother. The question was not; did it feel good; the question was, what was his duty? I hoped that I would never confront such a difficult situation, but I knew in my heart that I would have to deal with a thousand conflicts in my lifetime. Would I face them head-on and fight fairly, lovingly?

"Yes sir," I replied.

"I see in this young man's gut a fire—a fire that is stoked by justice and controlled by the damper of wisdom. I see a fire that burns brightly, not despite a loving heart, but because of it. I shall sign off on his graduation."

Emperor Charles V, the King, placed his scepter in my hand. "Are you prepared to lead, to scan the horizon with your eyes and your mind, to envision the future and to call upon your own Magician to conjure solutions to the challenges your followers face?"

"Yes, your excellency," I replied.

"Are you willing to call on your own Warrior to make the hard decisions? Do you have the will to enjoin others to follow you?"

"Yes, your excellency," I replied.

"Will you lead with courage, with wisdom, and with love?"

"Yes, your excellency," I replied.

"Bob is worthy of leadership," pronounced Charles V. "I shall sign off."

Mentor, who had been intently observing me throughout my examination by Warrior, Magician, and King, turned to Hans Sachs, the Lover. "It would appear that young Bob here has learned much that will sustain him on his life's journey. However, a journey is meaningless without a destination—a quest, if you will. My protégé, Bob, came to this place of Man's collective wisdom, in a quest for real love. Has he found it?"

Hans, with an uncharacteristically serious expression, stepped up to me and fixed me with an intense gaze. My eyes met that gaze with an earnest expression. The two young men, both deeply in love—Hans with Kunigunde and I with Gerdi—emanated energy; the *man cave* sparked and crackled like a roaring fire.

"Bob, you came to us infatuated—desperately in love, but not prepared to love—to really love as a man must if he is to bring happiness to his beloved. You had not unlearned the false lessons of your childhood. The tension in your birth family taught you to avoid, rather than confront conflict, to do what must be done. Your teachers' failure to see the potential masked by your speech impediment taught you to avoid challenging yourself intellectually. Rejection by your little friends taught you to depend on yourself, rather than to lead others to a common goal.

"Somehow, the overpowering experience of young love gave you the courage, the vision, and the will to ask for the hand of a woman in marriage."

"But she said '*nein!*'" I exclaimed.

"Yes," said Hans, "for she understood what you did not—that you were not ready for real love. By saying '*nein*' she protected herself—and you—from a lifetime of sorrow."

Mentor gently restated his earlier question: "Is he ready now?"

Hans, the archetype of Love, glanced knowingly at Mentor but turned the question to me. "Are you ready now, Bob?"

"I understand, from my apprenticeship with Warrior, that love must be strong, facing conflict head-on, managing the inevitable differences, and fighting fairly, lovingly."

The Hangman nodded.

"I understand from my apprenticeship with Magician, that my love must be curious about life in general and focus on a specific field of knowledge to provide for my loved ones. It is a lifelong process."

Hans Behaim smiled slightly but assumed a stern expression when I turned toward him. "Very good" was His only comment.

"I understand from my apprenticeship with King that that love must be anchored in *will*. A man without his own aspirations and the ability to inspire followers can neither provide direction to his family nor lead them to prosperity."

Charles V tapped his scepter.

"What is your decision, Hans, is he ready?" persisted Mentor.

Hans Sachs, the Lover, smiled and reverting to his Elvis persona, said, "Thank you, Boys; thank you very much." He then put an arm on my shoulder and turned to Mentor: "It's now or never..." he intoned, and I sang the next line:

"Come hold me tight..."

Mentor took up the chorus, and the whole gang joined in: "Tomorrow will be too late/It's now or never/My love won't wait..."

Now, with Charles V in the lead, we formed a conga line, snaked out of the Cobbler's shop, and danced down the narrow streets of Nuremberg. The King, Magician, Warrior, and Lover, with Mentor and me following, made quite a scene, dancing and singing in a strange tongue, but the staid *Bürgers* paid us no heed. Before long our gyrating procession reached a part of the old city wall familiar to me; it was where I had entered this sixteenth century backdrop for my initiation into manhood. I spotted the disturbed timbers partially concealing the opening from which I had emerged. To my surprise, Charles V, my King, led the conga line into the tunnel.

CHAPTER SEVENTEEN

The Light

Once I was engulfed by total blackness, I became aware of silence—and isolation. No longer was I dancing in a conga line and singing with Mentor and the others. The tunnel was familiar; was it five centuries—or five "moments" ago that I had been here, escaping from tormentors in the *SS Kaserne*? Then I had been frightened, but now I was calm. Then I had been confused, but now I knew what to do. Then I had been alone, but now I had a band of brothers within. I would emerge into the light a different and better man.

My Magician spoke to me. *Keep your right hand on the wall; no matter how many twists and turns the tunnel makes, you will eventually find your way.* That was good advice. Whenever my path led down a dead end, it returned to the main tunnel. With patience and faith in my Magician, I systematically made my way back to the lowest sub-basement of the *SS Kaserne* and the staircase that led to my "real" world, five floors above.

I hesitated; clearly, my perception of time had been altered by an excursion into the sixteenth century Nürnberg portion of Man's Collective Unconsciousness. Would I emerge from this psychological trip exactly where I had entered it—in the middle of a confrontation with a platoon of drunken infantrymen (infantry *boys*, really...) assuaging their feeling of homesickness on Christmas Eve by ganging up on other G.I.s? Had I returned safely from my apprenticeships with Franz Schmidt, the Hangman, Hans Behaim, the builder, Emperor Charles V, and Lover Hans Sachs, only to be beaten to a pulp by my twentieth-century "comrades"?

My Warrior made the decision. I knew what I had to do. I raced up the stairs to the *Kaserne's* first sub-basement, the lowest level soldiers

were permitted to use. I squeezed through the boards barring the stairwell, ran past the Quartermaster area, and climbed the remaining two
flights of stairs to my own platoon area. As I rounded the corner, I heard
a commotion down the hall, beyond the latrine. What now?

The voice of Charles V, my inner King, called to me: *Take charge, Bob!*

I burst into the Headquarters Troop orderly room, startling the Sp/4
pulling Charge of Quarters duty. "Wake up, Jack, we've got a situation!"

"I wasn't sleeping, Bob," said Jack Kovar, a radio operator from Commo Platoon, rubbing his eyes, "Was is los?"

The Officer of the Day, Lieutenant Biefert, looked up from the book
he had been reading. "What's the problem, soldier?"

"Big trouble, sir, twenty or so infantry boys beating up a Commo guy."

The O.D. summoned the Military Police, who arrived in minutes. I
led Lieutenant Biefert and the squad of MPs to the hallway outside my
room, where order was quickly restored. The drunken thugs, sobered by
well-placed police batons, lined up against the wall. Their bravado was
spent. One young man was crying.

Their victim, Private Zucho, lay bruised, one eye shut, and bleeding
from his nose. Medics from Headquarters Troop administered first aid
and brought a stretcher. Zucho would be transported to the Army hospital in Furth for x-rays and observation.

The offenders were handcuffed and marched off to a holding pen,
where they would spend their Christmas. Depending on Zucho's condition, they would face court martial or administrative punishment.

"Good work, soldier," the Officer of the Day told me, "your quick
thinking saved that fellow from further injury."

"Thank you, sir," I said.

"I am glad that you were not afraid to get involved. Some might fear
retribution, but I assure you that this bunch will not be returning to the
Second Cav."

"Very good, sir," I replied.

"I have enough information for a preliminary report, soldier. It's still
early; why don't you get out and celebrate Christmas Eve?"

"I didn't put in for a pass, sir; I had K.P. today."

"Well, you have one now. Get cleaned up, and pick it up from the
orderly room."

"Yes sir!"

After I showered and changed into civvies, I entered the orderly room. Jack Kovar handed me a freshly typed three-day pass, signed by Lieutenant Biefert. "The Lieutenant will let Sergeant Holmes know what happened," said Jack. "Have a good three days." Then he smiled and tilted his head: "Are you going to spend it with Gerdi?"

"I'll do my best, Jack," I said. "She knew I was on the duty roster, so she made plans to visit friends this evening. I know where she transfers streetcars though, and I'll try to intercept her on her way home."

"Good luck, Bob, and thanks for helping a fellow Commo guy!"

CHAPTER EIGHTEEN

A Second Chance

I waved to the MPs at the front gate as I walked out of the *Kaserne*. As usual, I ignored the line of black Mercedes-Benz cabs on *Allersberger Straße*. I normally preferred to walk, often for hours, rather than take cabs or the *Strassenbahn*. Christmas decorations in the city were festive but tasteful—no animated, dancing reindeer lit the streetlamps and apartment buildings along Allersberger Strßse. On the other side of the viaduct at the main train station, I followed the city wall to the large intersection and streetcar transfer point known as the *Plärrer*. Here, I knew, was where Gerdi would transfer streetcars on her way home from her visit with the Geigers, and here I would wait for her.

A cold drizzle pelted me, but I waited patiently. My reward would be the sight of Gerdi's face. An hour passed. Holiday revelers, arm in arm, passed the *Plärrer* singing, some waving bottles in their free hands. I scanned the faces alighting from every *Straßenbahn* entering the circular track surrounding the *Plärrer*. Rain dripping from my hair blurred my vision. My teeth chattered. I relished the temporary discomfort, feeling that it somehow affirmed my love for Gerdi.

Finally, at eleven PM, Gerdi stepped down from the streetcar. I glowed! *"Frohe Weihnachten, Schatzie,"* I said, embracing her.

"Frohe Weihnachten, Tweety," replied Geri, *"Was machts du hier?"* What are you doing here?

"The Army gave me a Christmas present—you!"

"Let us get you dried off," said Gerdi. "Come, here is our *Straßenbahn*."

"No, let's walk," I said. The rain had turned to light snow.

"Ja," okay Tweety," replied Gerdi, acquiescing to my unusually assertive decision. She looked at me with a strange expression, her head

tilted and her brows furrowed. We strolled arm in arm along the handsome city wall. Allied bombing had destroyed much of the old city of Nürnberg in 1945, but restoration had been a top priority of its citizens following the war. The wall had been rebuilt—not to its greatest glory, perhaps, but sufficiently to frame a onetime jewel in the Holy Roman Emperor's crown. Care had been taken to preserve the original architectural flavor within those walls and to restore churches and other public buildings as faithfully as possible. Civic pride runs deep in Nürnbergers—much deeper than the shame of their city's recent association with the Hitler regime. I stopped several times, gazing at the rooftops of the old city just beyond the wall.

"Is everything okay, Tweety?"

My faraway expression turned to a warm smile: "Yes, *Schatzie*, I was just thinking that you must be very proud of your heritage—this city."

"*Ja*, we learned all about it in school. Do you know that Nürnberg was very important in the Holy Roman Empire?"

"Yes. I read that each new emperor held his first diet in Nürnberg, as decreed by the Golden Bull."

"You are very clever, Tweety. You must read a lot when you work in the Army."

"Yes, it's a way to fill the long hours when I am away from you."

"Oh Tweety—*Quatschkopf!*" Yet, as she used that familiar term of endearment, meaning "silly," she immediately bowed her head, as though she regretted her use of that word, perhaps inappropriate for the strangely serious man walking with her on this snowy Christmas Eve.

We soon reached the *Hauptbahnhof*—the main train station. "People are still going in and out of the *Bahnhof*," I said.

"Of course, Bob," said Gerdi, "It never closes."

"Let us see if we can get something hot to eat there, and maybe some *Glühwein*," I suggested.

"Okay," said Gerdi. She seemed to be enjoying my take-charge behavior. She had told me once that she always found it exhausting to make decisions when we were together, for I usually agreed with whatever she said, just to please her.

Inside, the Bahnhof was surprisingly busy for the late hour on Christmas Eve. There were even train departures. As we munched *Nürnberger Bratwurst* and sipped hot spicy wine, I studied the mechanical departure board, clicking and clacking with every change. In the past, I had dismissed the complicated data display as beyond my comprehension, but now I felt sure that if I made a real effort I could decipher the train schedule.

"I don't have to report for duty until Monday evening," I told Gerdi, "and you will certainly be off Monday for Christmas."

"Since Christmas falls on Saturday this year, we have Monday and Tuesday off."

"December 26th is a holiday in Germany too?"

"Of course, so Tuesday is our holiday for that day."

"Well I have a little Christmas present for you, Schatzie, but we have to hurry. There's a midnight train to *München*."

Ten minutes later, the train pulled out of Nürnberg, picking up speed as it turned south to Munich. I, an American lad, and my German girlfriend laughed giddily in our compartment in the nearly empty train. We had no luggage, no toiletries, and no idea where we would stay when we arrived in the Bavarian Alps on Christmas.

The cavernous central train station of Munich was an eerie place at two o'clock Christmas morning. There were drunks, of course, but the *Polizei* did not bother them—better for them to be sleeping quietly in the waiting room than staggering in the street. One all-night snack counter was open, a refuge for holiday travelers who did not have carefully planned itineraries.

Two of those spontaneous souls, Gerdi and I, enjoyed every minute of that long winter's night. "When I was a little boy," I said, "I always tried to stay awake on Christmas Eve, so I could see Santa Claus."

"Did you ever see him?"

"No, I was always fast asleep by midnight, but my older brother, Lynn, swore that he saw Santa come in and leave presents under the tree."

"Did he come down the chimney?"

"No, we didn't have a fireplace, and the fat man would have gotten stuck in the smoke stack coming out of the oil stove in our living room. Lynn said that Santa came in through the front door."

"So when you woke up, there were presents for everyone!"

"Yes. We couldn't open them until my parents got up, though. It always seemed to take forever for my dad to go to the bathroom."

Gerdi laughed. "For us, Christmas is a little different. The big day is Christmas Eve, when the family gathers around the Christmas tree, and we exchange gifts."

"No Santa Claus?"

"We have an old fellow we call *St. Nikolaus…*"

"Old St. Nick!"

"Right—I think—he is more of a religious figure, with a golden cross and a big book with all the kids' names in it."

"Oh, and whether they were good or bad, that sort of thing?"

"Exactly. Of course, I was always good…"

"Of course," I teased.

"…so my shoes were filled with candy, fruit, and maybe a little toy."

"Did St. Nick come on Christmas Eve?"

"No, he has his own *St. Nikolaus Day,* December 6th."

And so, deeply in love and oblivious to the strangers around them, we whiled away the hours until dawn of Christmas Day, 1965. Fortified by strong coffee and *Brötchen* slathered with butter and strawberry jam, we deepened our understanding of each other, Gerdi speaking in German, and I responding in English. What a pair we made!

With the sunrise came activity in the Munich Hauptbahnhof: Other refreshment stands were unshuttered, the ticket windows opened, and diesel locomotives could be heard rumbling up to their assigned platforms. Holiday travelers flooded the station. Grandparents visiting from tiny villages, college students on school break, families heading to the countryside, and couples off to skiing holidays, studied the whirring mechanical announcement boards—train departures and arrivals. I noted the departure time for Salzburg. I knew from experience that we could reach our final destination by transferring at *Freilassing*, a little station stop on the Munich-Salzburg line. Gerdi caught up to me as I strode to the ticket window. "Where are we going, Tweety?" she asked me, unable to contain her curiosity.

"Zwei Karten nach Berchtesgaden," she heard me say at the ticket window.

"Berchtesgaden!" Gerdi knew about Berchtesgaden of course; everyone did. Its most infamous resident had been Herr Hitler. His *Berghof* on the *Obersalzberg* mountain above Berchtesgaden, where he and his mistress, Eva Braun, entertained famous visitors, held a commanding view of the Alps. Hitler and his henchmen planned many of their conquests from the Nazi complex on Obersalzberg. She also knew that the area had been taken over by the Americans at the end of the war and used for military recreation. German visitors were not welcome. "Are you sure it's okay for us to go there Tweety?"

"Sure, with my military I.D., we're in like Flynn. You are my guest." Actually, however, I was not completely sure, since we had no reservations.

* * *

"You're in luck, buddy," the desk clerk said when we finally arrived. "We had a cancellation, so there's one room available." He checked my I.D. and the pass signed by Lieutenant Biefert and handed me the key.

From our room we had a commanding view of the mountains and valleys surrounding us. We were on top of the world, literally and emotionally, but exhausted from our overnight journey, we soon collapsed in bed. "Merry Christmas, Schatzie" I said.

"Merry Christmas, Schatzie," she said, snuggling next to me.

Daylight was waning when we awoke. After making love, we explored the U.S. military recreation facilities. We wandered into the bar, and settling into a nook with spectacular Alpine views, we summoned the waiter. "We must try the *Weißbier*," suggested Gerdi, so we sipped cloudy, unfiltered wheat beer and munched on *Weißwurst*, or white sausage, with sweet mustard and rolls, a Bavarian favorite. Other G.I.s, mostly officers and non-commissioned officers, filled the Nazi-built resort, now one of the spoils of war for the U.S. government.

"How could Hitler have defiled such a beautiful place with his Nazi complex," wondered Gerdi aloud.

"I suppose he felt the need to get away from Berlin and make big decisions in an awesome setting," I said. "But," I added, gesturing to the majestic peaks, "these mountains are timeless. Hitler's mark was just an ugly smear that will be washed clean like rat scat covered by fresh snow. The mountains remain, and people will always come here to make important decisions."

Gerdi said nothing, but she smiled and blushed.

We caught the Army shuttle bus into town and walked the streets of Berchtesgaden arm in arm as Christmas candles flickered in windows. We window-shopped for gifts that neither of us could afford, but we derived much delight in our shared fantasies. "Someday…" I said. Gerdi just squeezed my hand.

Later, after an American-style Christmas feast at the resort—turkey, ham, yams, and cranberries, we wrapped ourselves in blankets from our bed and sat on the snow-covered balcony of our room. Church bells from the village below pealed through the cold night air. The sky was black velvet strewn with diamonds. Our bodies were warm, touching under the blanket. We held hands in silence. Tomorrow would be another day.

* * *

December 26th dawned clear and cold—and so did the young lovers, for we had left our blankets on the balcony the night before in our eagerness to climb into bed. The weather was just right, however, for a sleigh ride to *Konigssee*, a picturesque lake only three miles away. Traversing the deep, frozen lake, we gazed at the steep mountains towering 6,000 feet over the lake. Before us stood the charming *St. Bartolomä Church*, a cluster of simple, white cylinders, capped by onion shaped domes. Its vertical, yet modest arrangement seemed to kneel in homage to its majestic surroundings—a house of God made by man in a garden made by God.

"Let's find the priest and ask him to marry us!" I exclaimed.

"Quatschkopf," responded Gerdi, smiling, but with an edge to her voice, "let's just enjoy this magical Christmas." A dark cloud floated over Jenner Mountain, invading the blue heaven above us.

There was that word: Quatschkopf—silly. I knew what she meant; this would be our last Christmas together, for I would be mustered out of the Army in two months. We had been over all this before, when I offered her an engagement ring. She loved me, she had said, but she foresaw problems that could strangle young love and turn it into something terrible.

"You are young, and you have no experience with women," she told me. "You do not have an education or profession. You are sweet, Tweety, but a man must be more than sweet! He must be…strong," she told me. "We are from different worlds," she told me, "You are American, and I am German. Everything I know is here: my job, my friends, my things. How can I leave everything I have ever known to join you in America? How would we live? I could not work, and you have no profession."

I had been devastated when Gerdi turned down my proposal. I had no answers to her objections, but I could not imagine life without her. My despair had descended to the level of depression by Christmas Eve, when I found myself escaping from conflict into that terrible, long, black night beneath the *SS Kaserne*.

Gliding over the Koenigssee with Gerdi beside me under a warm blanket, I experienced a sudden insight. I understood why I had taken that incredible journey to sixteenth century Nürnberg, why I had met and been apprenticed to the Warrior, the Magician, the King, and the Lover. Each of those spirits—for they were surely spirits—represented energy centers within me that had yet to be realized. Gerdi had sensed that immaturity in me intuitively; she understood that I was not ready to step into the role of husband and father. But I now knew something that Gerdi did not know; I *had* taken that journey. I *had* learned from the best. I *was* ready.

I squeezed Gerdi's hand as if to reassure her that she need not concern herself with my impetuous suggestion about the charming *St. Bartolomä Church* on the Koenigssee. I smiled at her, and she smiled back.

In the mountains, weather can change suddenly. By the time we returned to our hotel, a snowstorm was raging. We stamped our shoes outside and entered the main lobby, warmed by the glow of its huge fireplace. It would be a cozy den for us to enjoy the remaining hours of our Christmas getaway. Tomorrow the train would take us back to Nürnberg—and reality.

CHAPTER NINETEEN

The Final Word

Gerdi and I sat before the roaring fireplace alone, for many of the officers and NCOs had left Berchtesgaten by Sunday evening. Our eyes were fixed on the flames, but our thoughts were elsewhere.

"You seem different, somehow," said Gerdi, "but is it just because it is Christmas, and we are in such a beautiful place?"

"Is this it?" I said. "Will we take the train back to Nürnberg tomorrow and let our love fizzle out over the next two months?"

"You are so sweet," said Gerdi, "a nice boy. You'll go home, find a nice American girl, and forget about your *Schatzie*, your first love."

I thought of Hans Sachs, the Lover. Would he allow this intense feeling to peter out, to become only a sweet memory? No! He would never give up on love—and neither will I.

"Still," said Gerdi, "you will make someone a good husband. Too bad that someone will not be me."

A voice spoke to me; it was the Warrior, saying, *you must fight for love! A man's gotta do what a man's gotta do.*

"If only you could convince me that this could work," said Gerdi. "I don't know how two people from such different backgrounds could find happiness in the long run…"

Think, young man! Use that head of yours! It was Hans Behaim, the Magician. *You know her concerns are logical: the language difference, the differences between your history and culture and hers. The job situation, man! How can you support a wife? What if she is unhappy in the United States? Then what? Nürnberg is a long way from Chicago. She would be stuck.*

"Those are great questions, Herr Behaim," I thought. "Do you have answers for me?"

* * *

Look within, Bob to your own Magician. Everything you need is there.
"The fire feels good, doesn't it?"
"*Ja*," replied Gerdi, taking my hand.
"The pot roast was great."
"*Ja*, I like some American food."
"Would you care for another glass of wine?"
"*Ja*, that would be good."
I returned with two glasses of *Gluhwein*. "Hot wine for a cold night," I said.
"*Danke schön*, Schatzie."
We sipped our hot, spiced wine and gazed at the fire.

* * *

I wrestled with my Magician: "How can we make this work?" I focused on the flames and allowed my mind to relax. *Nearer to Thee, my God...*

Thoughts leaped out of the flames in fragments. Elements of a plan arranged themselves before me like the architectural features of the Holy Ghost Hospital on Hans Behaim's drawings. I allowed those elements to bubble up from my unconsciousness and take shape on the drawing table of my mind. I studied them and rearranged them like pieces of a jigsaw puzzle. They fit together perfectly.

* * *

"Thank you," I said aloud.
"Schatzie, *you* brought the wine glasses, remember?"
"Oh yes, Gerdi, I meant thank you for making this a wonderful Christmas."
"*Frohe Weihnachten*, Schatzie,"
"Merry Christmas, Schatzie."
We lapsed into silence again.

* * *

I knew I had a workable plan, a plan that would permit us to give in to our emotions, a plan that would assuage Gerdi's fears—a plan for our future life together. I went over and over the plan as the fire burned and the other remaining guests retired to their rooms.

* * *

"I will always remember this night, Schatzie," said Gerdi. "I will never forget you."

* * *

"Oh God," I thought, "she's thinking about a future without me already. This is my last chance; it's now or never. But what if I'm wrong? What if she doesn't agree?"

A leader leads, Bob. It was Charles V speaking. *If you are sure you are right, be strong. If you are a good man, the people will follow.*

* * *

"Gerdi, we have to talk."

"Okay, Tweety, what do you want to talk about?"

"For now, honey, let's can the 'Tweety.' I want you to listen very carefully. Let's stretch our legs."

We rose from our comfortable chairs by the fire and strolled over to the window overlooking the mountains and the valleys. The black sky was filled with stars.

"What is it, Schatzie? You seem so serious!"

"Do you love me, Gerdi?"

"You know I do, Bob."

"Then promise to marry me."

Gerdi began to cry softly. "Do you think this is easy for me Schatzie? I do love you! But you have no idea what it all means…"

"Yes I do, Gerdi. Believe me, I have given this a lot of thought. First, I must know that you truly love me. The rest is a matter of details."

"Of course I love you, Bob. Tell me what you are thinking."

I outlined my plan. I would go home in two months, at my elapsed time of service. I would attend electronics school full-time on the G.I. Bill, attaining a marketable skill in twelve months. During that year, Gerdi would use some of her vacation time to visit me in Chicago. The impressions she gained would govern our next step. If it were favorable, she would apply for an immigration visa. Upon graduation, I would seek gainful employment as an electronics technician. Assured that my income would support us, Gerdi would request a one-year furlough from her job and join me. We would be married and live in the States for one year. Only then would we decide whether to remain in America or return to Germany. During our first year of married life, I would study German, so that I would be qualified to work as an electronics technician in Germany.

Gerdi listened intently. Her expression brightened as I supplied details of my plan.

"You have really given much thought to your plan, Schatzie. We do not go crazy and shut doors. We have a chance."

"It will be difficult to be away from you," I said, "but we would be working toward a future together."

"*Ja...*"

"It would be a test of our commitment."

"*Ja...*"

I knelt and took her hand. The window above my head framed black velvet, mountain sky, sprinkled with starry points of possibility. "Gerdi, will you marry me?"

Her answer, Alex, my beloved grandson, the answer your dad's mother gave me, made my entire ordeal in that alien world worthwhile—the lessons of which I fervently wish to impart to you as you step onto the stage of Manhood:

* * *

Gerdi's eyes glowed as she knelt beside me, and taking both of my hands in her own, replied in a voice trembling with emotion, "Ja...Ja! Yes!"

The Author and Gerdi

Afterword

"**W**ow, Grandpa, that really is an amazing story! Is it true? Did you get hit on the head or something and experience hallucinations?"

"Okay, Alex, let's just say the story you just heard is part fact, part fiction, and a lot of wishful thinking—lessons learned over a lifetime that I *wish* I had mastered at your age. But this I tell you, my beloved grandson, every word of it contains truth—truth from my past and truth for your future. Marry her, Alex; love her, and take care of her with the help of your own Warrior, Magician, King, and Lover."

"I will, Grandpa."

"I love you Alex," said the old man.

"I love you too," said the young man.

Ode to a Cottonwood Tree

Born of a wild seed, carried by the wind,
You appeared;
It was love at first sight.

Transplanted to strange land,
You took root;
You brought forth new life.

Shade in the summer, rustling leaves,
I recall, through it all,
The good times.

Autumn is the season you went away,
Dropping leaves
That I gathered with a prayer.

All through the winter, I longed to feel
Your return,
In your shade, in the snow.

Springtime reminds me, you are always near;
You awake,
And your seed is everywhere.

Seasons, and the years turn,
And I leave this land.
You remain in this place in my heart.

Ich liebe dich noch, Schatzie.

Tweety

Acknowledgements

This attempt to transmit some of the lessons life has taught me is drawn from everyone I have known and from the wisdom of the ages bound in time by the written word.

Written sources that were particularly important to me are listed as "For Further Reading" at the back of this book. The concepts of "King," "Warrior," "Magician," and "Lover" are from the work of Robert Moore, and Douglas Gillette. The interpretation of these terms is my own. I apologize for any misinterpretation and encourage readers to explore *King, Warrior, Magician, Lover: Rediscovering the Archetypes of the Mature Masculine*. Most of my understanding of *Nuremberg in the Sixteenth Century* comes from Gerald Strauss' wonderful book of that title.

Many thanks to students of Oak Lawn Community High School, in Oak Lawn, Illinois, who in 2005 and 2006, brainstormed questions that they would ask Franz Schmidt, Hans Behaim, Charles V, and Hans Sachs if they were apprenticed to those historical figures, as was the protagonist of this novel.

I greatly appreciate the members of the Lug-ins-Land Lions Club of Nürnberg, whose hospitality deepened my appreciation of the city and its people during my 2011 research trip for this book.

The love of Gerdi and our two sons, Michael and Richard; my wife, Barbara and children, Ken and Christina; our wonderful grandchildren, and my birth family motivated this love story.

Special thanks go to Janet Potter, whose careful editing spared readers numerous typos; and Mike Potter, whose design skills and technological magic turned a simple manuscript into this attractive publication.

For Further Reading

Campbell, Joseph (1971). *The Portable Jung*. New York: Viking Penguin.

Covey, Stephen (1989). *The Seven Habits of Highly Effective People: Restoring the Character Ethic*. New York: Free Press.

Holy Bible.

Jung, Carl, (1961). *Memories, Dreams, Reflections*. New York: Random House.

Keller, Albrecht (ed.), 1928. *A Hangman's Diary: Being the Journal of Master Franz Schmidt, Public Executioner of Nuremberg, 1573-1617*. London: Philip Allan & Co. LTD.

Milton, John (1608-1674). *Paradise Lost*.

Moore, Robert and Gillette, Douglas (1990). *King, Warrior, Magician, Lover: Rediscovering the Archetypes of the Mature Masculine*. New York: HarperCollins.

Shakespeare, William (1564-1616). *King Lear*.

Strauss, Gerald (1966). *Nuremberg in the Sixteenth Century*. New York: John Wiley & Sons.

www.ingramcontent.com/pod-product-compliance
Lightning Source LLC
Chambersburg PA
CBHW052137170626
46812CB00004B/1475